KEEP YOUR FRIENDS CLOSE
AND YOUR FRENEMIES CLOSER.

FRENEMIES

NICOLE
BLANCHARD

NEW YORK TIMES & USA TODAY
BESTSELLING AUTHOR

Frenemies

Copyright © 2019 by Nicole Blanchard

Bolero Books LLC
11956 Bernardo Plaza Dr. #510
San Diego, CA 92128
www.buybolerobooks.com

CONTENTS

DEDICATION

To my gypsies Rachel, Sara, and Lisa.
Because family don't end in blood.

CHAPTER ONE

LAYLA

"WHAT DO you mean I have to take another class?" I demanded. "I'm on schedule to graduate in the spring. I've satisfied all the requirements for both my business and art majors."

My advisor, Ms. Jensen, a harried woman in her mid-fifties with her hair always in a bun and her lipstick always smeared, took off her glasses and wiped them with the hem of her wrinkled cardigan. "Ms. Tate, one of the general business classes you took at another facility do not transfer to our institution. It seems previous advisors were not aware, and therefore, you weren't informed. However, if you want to graduate with your degree in business, you'll need to take another business elective and the only one available is Business Ethics. The last available opening is at eight on Monday, Wednesday, and Friday mornings. It'll put you at five classes for the semester, but with your academic record, I don't anticipate it being an issue."

I slumped back in my seat, my brain racing. I'd prepared my

schedule with a fastidiousness bordering on obsession over the last three years. I had to if I wanted to graduate on time with my double major and keep my mother off my back.

I didn't just want to graduate this spring—I needed to.

Not only to prove to myself I made the right choice to pursue art in addition to her business degree requirement, but to prove it to my mother that a menial, low-income position like art was a good career move, even if it didn't feel like it at the moment. If I'd gone into finance like she'd wanted me to, I could have secured an entry-level position making quadruple what I'd make as an artist starting out.

But finance wasn't what got me up in the morning. It wasn't what made my blood pump and my nerves trill as I anticipated the next piece I could tackle or the next aspiring artist I could inspire. In other words—I'd never be my mother—and I'd never be able to make her happy.

Learning I hadn't worked hard enough to be on top of my credits was only going to prove her right and *that* wasn't a conversation I was looking forward to.

"This has to be some sort of mistake. I've triple-checked my credits and degree requirements ever year." Was it hot? I was sweating. My legs were sticking to the leather seats.

"I'm sorry, Ms. Tate, but my hands are tied." She reaches across the expanse of the desk between us to hand me a folder fat with paperwork. "This is all the information you'll need to know about the class. Dates, schedules, syllabus. Your first class will be Wednesday morning at eight."

My eyes nearly popped right out of my head. "Ms. Jensen,"

I glanced at the first sheet, "is there no way to accept the transfer credit? Five classes in addition to my part-time job is a lot to juggle. Is there no way to dispute the ruling?"

Ms. Jensen, who'd lived and breathed administration for the past thirty years merely smiled, getting to her feet. "You're a bright girl, Layla. I'm sure you won't have any problem figuring out the details. If you'll excuse me, I have a ten o'clock."

Thoroughly dismissed, and frankly at a loss for words, I got to my feet and wordlessly shook Ms. Jensen's hand. She was already turning to leaf through paperwork as I drug my feet to the hallway. There wasn't a day during my college career where I'd been as dejected as I was leaving her office. My heart thudded in my chest like it was about to call it quits, my arms hung listless by my side, my fingers barely retaining their grip on the folder. What was the point? It was a stupid thing to be upset over, but I wanted to start the semester on a positive note, and this absolutely wasn't it.

I'd worked so hard, *so hard*, the past few years to do the right things, for my future, and to impress my mother.

I guess I'd have to work a little bit harder.

THAT WEDNESDAY before my first Business Ethics class, I considered throwing in the towel completely. I could go backpacking. Off the grid. I snorted. It wouldn't matter. My mother would still find me. If I didn't answer my cell phone on her first call, she would just keep calling.

"If you would have listened to me, you'd have a prestigious position at the firm waiting for you in the spring after graduation," she said.

"Uh huh," I answered automatically. I winced at my mother's screech in my ear. Normally, I'd give her an explanation guaranteed to placate her when she worked herself into a state, but I was already late for my first day of the new class, and I didn't have the time to muster up any patience to finesse her into a better mood.

"Are you even listening to me?" Her voice was like nails stabbing into my ears. "I swear you are the most ungrateful child on this earth. I've given you everything, my time, my money, even my body, and this is how you repay me. Your sister never treated me like this. She was always such a good girl."

With the implication being that I wasn't.

It wasn't the first time I'd heard how much I'd failed as a Tate. According to my mother, I couldn't do anything right. "I'm listening, Mother," I responded as I hustled my way across campus. Parking was such a joke. It was my senior year and I should have mastered how to find a spot and get to class on time by now. I could only hope the professor didn't have a stick up his ass.

The truth was, I'd let Mom work me up into such a state I missed my entrance to campus and had to double back. Traffic was a nightmare, as it is every morning on Tennessee Street, and it took double the time to turn around and fight my way to the parking garage. A headache had begun to make itself known so I stopped off to Einstein's for a bagel and coffee to ward it off. All the while my mother shrieked in my ear about her favorite topic: how I was a complete and utter failure to her.

"You could have fooled me. I asked you if you'd given any thought to the position I forwarded to your email."

I chugged the coffee and cursed viciously under my breath when some of it splashed on the crisp white button-up shirt I'd bought specifically for my first day of senior year. That's what I got for trying to pretend to be a professional. Unlike my older sister Delia, I couldn't quite seem to pull off the effortless elegance. I was more a harried homebody.

"I haven't had time to check," I answered, despite knowing that wasn't the response she was looking for. It didn't matter what I said. I could do everything exactly the way she wanted it and she would still find a reason to complain.

"Layla Lucille, the firm is expecting your response." My mother had a habit of emphasizing random words in the middle of a conversation when she was especially incensed by my idiocy. "Please make it a point to respond to the job posting by the end of business today or you will lose this opportunity."

She didn't have to say she'd be disappointed. She was perpetually disappointed. Besides, she made it a point to call me no less than three times a day to check on my progress. Three years ago, I sent her in to apoplectic fits of rage when I changed my major from finance to art with a minor in education. No amount of threats or intimidation could sway me to change my mind. In the end, I compromised and double-majored in business and art to get her off my back. It meant more work for me, but I'm used to work. It also meant less free time, but other than my best friends Charlie and Ember, I didn't really have many social commitments. Besides, I could use the business side to manage my career in the future.

It still burned my ass that mother got her way in any respect, but I only had one more year to suffer through her meddling, and then I would be free. I'd have my degree, could get a respectable job, and be out from underneath her thumb. May seemed like an eternity from now, but as long as I kept focused, I'd make it through.

"I'll take a look at it after classes," I said. Before she could object, I pushed through the lecture hall doors and added, "Class is about to start. I have to go."

If it was possible to shame someone over the phone, Magdalene Bennett Tate was able to do it. "I expect to hear from you the moment you answer the position posting this evening."

"I'll talk to you later," I said instead of answering. She didn't know it, but I had no intention of applying for the position. I may have been graduating with a degree in business, but I had no desire to join her friend's firm, no matter how many tantrums she threw.

She disconnected without saying another word and in that way, it made her feel like she controlled the conversation.

Stomach full of lead from yet another stress-filled conversation before 9:00 a.m., I could no longer stomach the thought of eating my onion bagel with cream cheese. Full of remorse, I tossed it in the trash can before navigating upstairs to the lecture hall. Business Ethics was one of the last courses I'd need to complete the business degree and was only offered at the earliest slot in the morning. If my mom wasn't trying to kill me, my grueling schedule sure was.

I pushed through the doors to the lecture hall, hoping it will be a relatively easy A. The small group of students turned to face me, and the professor's voice cut off mid-sentence. So much for sneaking in unnoticed. Viscerally aware of their stares, I hurried with my eyes on my shoes to the first available desk at the back of the class. My cheeks began to burn as I pulled out my notebook and pencils. Having always been the perfect student, any sort of infraction made me incredibly uneasy.

"If that's the last interruption," came the professor's smooth, somewhat familiar male voice. He began to go over the syllabus and I followed along with the printed copy I pulled from my carefully organized binder.

My neck ached from the struggle to keep my eyes on my papers. I wanted to glance up to see who it was since my class list had the space for the professor blank the last time I checked, and I wondered if I'd taken one of their classes before. At the same time, if I knew them, I didn't want the shame of seeing the disappointment on their face, not so soon after the verbal lashing from my mother.

"Why don't we go down the rows and introduce ourselves?" he said, and I mentally groaned. Why teachers thought it was an important part of class, I'd never know.

When it was my turn, I finally looked up and promptly wished I hadn't. I manage to introduce myself, giving my name and major, but I don't know how.

All the while he smirked at me like he was enjoying my

discomfort.

He probably was, the immoral, no-good bastard.

My ears burned with indignation and embarrassment. The asshole probably didn't even care that I was late, he just wanted to see me squirm. As he went down the line of students, I pulled open my class schedule to confirm my suspicions, and noted the updated listing with growing horror: Business Ethics - D. Hampton, T.A.

Our gazes connected over the heads of the other students and heat crackled between us. It was the heat from fissures in the ground between us, because I must be in hell.

My goal for the past fifteen years of my life, aside from appeasing my mother, has been to annihilate Dashiel "Dash" Hampton. Ever since he humiliated me in front of the entire elementary school during the spelling bee.

I narrowed my eyes at him, thankful no one could see the war waging between us since I was at the back of the room. He merely continued teaching as though my presence didn't bother him. Fine. Two could play that game. If it didn't bother him, then I wouldn't let him see how much it bothered me.

Despite the conscious effort I made to keep my eyes on my paper where I took notes on his expectations for the semester and the timeline of papers and assignments to be due, I couldn't help but glancing back up at him when I didn't think he was looking. Of all the classes in all the lecture halls in all the buildings on campus, I got the one where Dash was the T.A. or, as he said in his introduction, "Call me Mr. Hampton." I barely managed to control my responding snort.

Mr. Hampton. I bet he was loving that.

It would be a cold day in hell before I ever called him Mr. Hampton.

Class continued uneventfully, unless I counted the times I glanced up from my notes to find Dash smirking down at me. I ground my teeth and reminded myself I couldn't hit a teacher, even if he was a T.A., and tried to focus on the information he was presenting. It didn't help that each time our gazes connected, I was hit with a wave of irritation so strong, I wanted to launch myself from my seat and wipe that smirk off his face.

The moment the hour was up, I thrust myself out of the desk, but not in his direction. In fact, I hustled toward the door like he was my mother trying to set me up with a sweet boy she knew from church.

"Ms. Tate?" I heard him call before I could reach freedom.

I spun around and slammed into a wall of muscled chest.

This couldn't be happening.

Taking a generous step back, I straightened my shoulders and tried to pretend like I was as unaffected as he looked. "Yes?"

He was close enough that I could see the flecks of darker green in his mossy colored eyes, and I noted that he was weeks overdue for a haircut. As long as I'd known him, he'd been fastidious about his appearance, so I knew the slightly messy, unkempt style must be intentional. Unlike me, Dash looked good no matter what time of the day. I remembered my stained shirt and hugged my books in front of my chest. His plaid button-up was perfectly pressed, and his jeans looked as if they'd just come off the rack.

The silence stretched on, but I refused to meet his gaze. If I was going to survive this semester with him, I would going to have to pretend like his stupid face didn't make me want to plant my fist in it. I'm sure there was something in the code of conduct forbidding assault on a staff member.

As I counseled myself to remember our new dynamic, his scent wrapped around me, catching me unaware and unprepared. Like warm sugar and smooth, dark whiskey it seeped into my system like a drug, and I found myself swaying forward for another taste.

"Ms. Tate?" he repeated, and the amusement in his voice had me snapping out of my stupor.

I looked up and found his smirk had been replaced by a slightly befuddled smile. "I'm sorry," I said, cursing myself for my stupidity. "What?"

"I hope you'll pay better attention in class, but I wanted to remind you that class starts at 8:00 am. I know it's early, but I hope you'll be on time in the future."

Oh, he was loving this. He had to be. I couldn't entirely blame him. If I had the chance to be in a position of power, I'd take it out on him, too.

"You bet," I replied through gritted teeth. "I have to get to my next class."

"I look forward to seeing you next time!" he called out to my back.

I made a mental note to check over the attendance policy. I'd never been the type of person to skip a class, but for Dash, I'd be willing to make an exception.

CHAPTER TWO

DASH

THE LONG AND short of it: I was fucked.

The last person I expected to see walk in to my classroom was the one woman I've wanted as long as I could remember.

It was just too bad she was the only woman who had never wanted me back.

I'd been a couple years ahead of her at the school we both attended, and each time she turned me down, it only made me more interested. I was convinced I'd begun wearing her down—until the day I beat her at the spelling bee.

I gathered my papers up and began readying myself for another class as I recalled the day. I'd been in fifth grade, Layla had been in third. We were both finalists in the spelling bee and even though she was a couple years younger, I'd been drawn to her. Back then it was because she also liked to read comics. Later, I learned it was because she liked the art, but I'd been a kid and knowing a girl who liked comics was out of the realm cool at the time. I only joined the damn spelling bee because I wanted to impress her. When she royally shot me down to share comics the day before, I figured if I couldn't have her, then I'd enjoy pissing her off.

After the spelling bee, there was the honor society elections, then student government, and class ranks. I'd been valedictorian of my graduating class. She made salutatorian. Nothing cheered up my day quite like pissing her off.

Except now she was my student, and there were just some lines I couldn't cross, but damn if I didn't want to toe the fuck out of them.

I made it through my subsequent classes on autopilot and headed straight to the gym to work the thought of Layla Tate out of my mind. Much as I wanted her beneath me, there wasn't anything I could do about it while she was my student. And wasn't that a fucking shame?

She was the type of woman who held everything together, who had her shit together. She didn't care, for the most part, about stuff like status, or money, like most of the women I knew. She cared about books, her art, her future. Stupid as it sounded, she inspired me to be a better person at a time in my life when I had no direction, no positive influence. If it hadn't been for her, who knows what the hell would have happened?

But I knew underneath that carefully buttoned and tightly wound exterior there was an absolute wildcat underneath. She may think we just had a rivalry, but it was so much more than that. She wanted to shove her foot up my ass and I wanted to shove my cock in her mouth.

An hour in the gym did little to help my dilemma, and I knew the past years of antagonization would have nothing on the upcoming months. I just had to keep it together long enough to finish the semester.

Should be easy enough.

* * *

THREE WEEKS later and I was losing my mind.

No amount of lifting weights in the gym or throwing myself in my grad work could erase her from my mind as easily as I'd forgotten other women. It's almost as bad as it had been in high school. I get a twenty-four-hour reprieve, forty-eight at the most, and then she was back in my class with those blue eyes on me, and I'd have to start all over again.

She was making me lose my fucking mind.

I'd pulled every trick in my arsenal to get her to see me as anything other than an enemy, but nothing worked. Now that I was her teacher? I might as well kiss any chance with her goodbye.

Women always came easy for me. That was never the problem. It was their motivation and scheming that always bit me in the ass. They were the ones who were only interested in my looks or my bank account. As cliché as it sounded, I wanted someone who didn't give a damn about those things. Someone who saw me for me and not for what they could *get* from me.

With Layla, it was never that easy. She didn't swoon at my looks and she wasn't impressed by my father or my trust fund. When I got a brand-new Camaro for my sixteenth birthday and came to school thinking I was God's gift, she rolled her eyes and disappeared to the library. I'll admit, it could be a little irritating. She thought I was shallow, vain, and an idiot. If I were a smart man, I'd forget her and focus on finishing my MBA without the distractions.

She'd agree, and I was starting to, that I was not a smart man.

"People are inherently altruistic," she stated in an argument with another student. "According to research, the human race is a stronger one if we work together to our mutual benefit. Therefore, most businesses are essentially naturally ethical because it's in their best interests to be so."

I turned to her and said, "Then you don't agree with economist Adam Smith who stated everyone should pursue their own selfish interests as it works out to the benefit of all as though guided by an invisible hand, Ms. Tate."

Definitely not a smart man.

She leaned back in her seat, the thrust of her back emphasizing the perfect upturn of her sweet breasts. I was going to hell.

"I do agree with him," she said, her eyes flashing, "because it was also Adam Smith who said human behavior is guided by self-interest as well as empathy. In fact, he believed self-interest was an engine of an economic system, but he also said it was a danger. Therefore, I still believe empathy and ethical behavior are the cornerstones of any economic system or business."

I pushed off my desk at the front of the room. "Can you give me an example from last week's readings of another economist or philosopher with similar ideas?"

Her blue eyes narrowed in my direction, scenting the challenge. Knowing she couldn't resist it, I could only try to hide my smile of satisfaction. "Chinese philosopher Mencius, for example, posited the innate human capacity for altruism in the child in danger scenario. He said, 'Suppose you're walking down the street and you come across the child about to fall into a hole. A human wouldn't worry about the cost of altering their plans for saving the child, they'd just do it automatically.'" Layla eyed me up and down. "Well, most humans."

We locked eyes for a moment, before she lowered hers down to her textbook. She couldn't have made that more clear, and I made it a point to focus on the other students for the remainder of the class. When it was over, I pinned her with my gaze. "Ms. Tate, a word."

The rest of the students filed out as Layla began to stuff her things into her bag. She stalked to my desk at the front.

"What?" she asked.

"I think you mean 'What, Mr. Hampton?'" I corrected.

She scoffed, "Is there something else? I've been on time every day and I haven't missed an assignment, clearly."

"Look, I don't want each class to be like a battlefield. We both have a job to do here, and I don't want this animosity between us to affect your grade." I wasn't thinking of how good she looked, or how much I wished I could bend her over the desk between us.

Layla shifted from foot to foot and tried to look innocent, but her smirk gave her away. "What animosity?"

"Cut the shit," I said while imagining her ass pink and splotchy from a good spanking. She'd like it. She'd look over her shoulder at me as I spanked her raw and she'd be spitting mad, but she'd egg me on until she was so sensitive, she couldn't sit without the accompanying sting.

Christ. I had to get her to leave my class before I did something stupid.

"All I want to do is finish this class so I can graduate in the spring. As long as you don't give me any trouble, I won't have a problem with my grade."

"Believe it or not, I'm not here to sabotage your grade. No matter what you may think of me, I do want you to pass this class," I said between gritted teeth. If I didn't have her splayed across my lap by the end of this semester, it'd be a miracle.

"Yeah, right. You've had it out for me ever since the fifth grade."

Unable to resist, I said, "Millennium," and watched her face flush with indignation. Of course, I'd rather it flushed for other reasons, but I'd take what I could get...for now.

"I hate you."

"You know what they say about love and hate."

"That it's a thin line between accidental death and premeditated murder," she retorted over her shoulder as she walked away.

I didn't watch her ass, and my mind didn't wander.

Much.

CHAPTER THREE

LAYLA

IT HAD ONLY BEEN a month and senior year was ruined.

My resting bitch face game was strong as I pulled into the parking lot of my apartment complex. Before I got out of the car, I was inundated with a wave of loneliness. I hadn't even gotten inside, and it already felt too empty. And it wasn't even because it was the weekend. No, it felt empty because the three amigas were down a number. I was happy for Charlie, she'd snagged a great place across town and closer to work, but that didn't mean it wasn't a punch in the chest each time I thought of running upstairs to the old place she used to rent before it was ruined, and she moved in with Liam.

Sometimes you just needed a shoulder.

I didn't like to show it, but I needed a shoulder today.

Rocky Road ice cream was in order. I decided. Maybe even a full pint instead of the half serving I normally allowed myself.

I wasn't overweight, but my body seemed to pack on the pounds at the slightest indulgence. I didn't have a problem with being extra curvy, but in addition to my mother's padded bank account, she also boasted extra padding everywhere else. No amount of money could make that woman say no to extra servings. Finance wasn't the only aspect of her I didn't want to emulate.

I should really stop accepting her calls. They never helped and always left me feeling worse.

The three-story apartment building Charlie, Ember—my other best friend—and I shared was located just off-campus. It had been the perfect place for the three of us during our years at Florida State University, for the first time, it didn't feel like home. I attributed it to lingering discontent from another bad phone call with my mom—certainly not from the constant clashing with Dash—and went straight for the freezer as soon as I got to my apartment.

My place wasn't much to speak of. Two sparse rooms, a bathroom, kitchen and meager living room. The whole square footage didn't amount to much, but it was enough for me, and Mom had offered to cover the rent since I was only working part time. What it lacked in amenities, the location sure made up for. That and the fact that for the past couple years, my two best friends had been a couple steps or an elevator ride away.

The reminder of Charlie not being there anymore had me digging into the chocolate-y goodness with renewed vigor. I still had Ember. I was making a bigger deal out of Charlie leaving than I needed to. Everything was just changing, and I didn't do well with changes. I liked consistency. Plans. Outlines. Lists. I still hadn't recovered from learning Dash was my T.A. That was absolutely something I hadn't anticipated.

Then again, Dash always pushed my buttons and disrupted my carefully laid plans.

After I finished with my ice cream, my plan was to go to my favorite place—the library—and figure out my next move. I needed to research the finance firm Mom was so adamant about and figure out if it was even something I was interested in. God knew I loved her, but I didn't want to spend my life in finance. Even though I'd turned her down weeks ago, she wasn't letting up. Maybe if I worked at the firm for a few years, I could use the time to allow my art to get off the ground. Then, I could explain to Mom in concrete examples how I could be successful in such a "useless profession."

With my goal in mind, and as I scooped another spoonful into my mouth, I began writing down a list. By the time I finished, I also polished off the ice cream. Considering that, I added GO TO THE GYM at the bottom and then went to throw out the trash and grab a bottle of water. I changed into a pair of gym sweats, a ratty T-shirt, and some old sneakers. Even if I could afford the tricked-out gym gear, I didn't get the point of dressing up in new clothes if I was just going to be soaked in sweat anyway.

Mood buoyed by the sugar and a loose plan, I practically skipped out into the hallway, where I ran smack dab into the last person in the world I wanted to see.

The world was conspiring against me. That was the only explanation.

Either that or he was stalking me, which had to be against university ethics on some level.

"Hey there, Ms. Tate." His voice was like warm caramel and was as satisfying as slipping into a warm bubble bath.

My eyes narrowed. "Dash."

He smirked. It had only been a month and I was already over being in his class. I couldn't wait until he was no longer my T.A. and I could wipe that smirk off his face. "I thought we agreed you'd call me Mr. Hampton?"

Through gritted teeth, I said, "The only way you'll ever hear me call you Mr. Hampton is if I suffer from a stroke," then turned and stalked away. I had to put up with him during class. I didn't have to put up with him outside of it. Then it occurred to me...he didn't live here. I stopped, turned. "What are *you* doing here?"

He lifts a hand to his chest. "Layla, I'm hurt. You sound disappointed to see me."

"I'm always disappointed to see you." Damn, what a waste of ice cream. My sugar high was already disappearing at the mere sight of him. "You didn't answer my question."

Dash, Mr. I'll-Never-Call-Him-Hampton couldn't look smugger. "You didn't ask nicely, but I'm in a charitable mood." Then he said the words that had my previously buoyed mood plummeting from put-on-big-girl-panties to set-panties-on-fire. "I live here."

My mouth became temporarily glued shut. I might have

choked on my own tongue. Some unladylike sounds later, I squawked, "*Live* here. Live where?"

"A room opened up upstairs. New renovation, too. I moved in at the start of the semester. Frankly, I'm hurt you didn't notice. And after we've had such a good time in class."

"You've got to be joking," I blurted. *Why* hadn't Charlie thought to tell me the bane of my existence was moving into her old place?

"'Fraid not, sweet cheeks."

My confusion was obliterated by rage and I saw a mist of red. "Don't call me sweet cheeks. I'm pretty sure that's against code of conduct, *Dash*."

His gaze lingered on my bared skin, which I had to be imagining. The thought of Dash, of all people, ogling me was laughable. He was probably searching for weak spots. "What do I have to do to get you to call me Mr. Hampton, just once?" he asked, and my thoughts were wrenched from his eyes on my skin.

"Drop dead?" I replied with exaggerated sweetness. I resorted to imagining him in various stages of embarrassment and ruin, which always used to cheer me up. Except now that he was in my personal space, my sanctuary, I felt even more exposed and I wished I was wearing something more substantial...like a parka. The way he was looking at me, it was almost like I was naked. Which is absurd. Dash liked to torture me—and not in any pleasurable sort of way.

My brain—probably high on chocolate and his cologne—connected the thought of pleasure with Dash, who was standing way too close for comfort. First, I imagined him running naked through the quad, with the whole campus laughing at him. It would serve him right, the bastard. Except, the image shifted, and then he was naked, and we were alone.

And no one was laughing, least of all me.

As though he could read my mind, Dash chuckled, those clear green eyes crinkling at the corners. His parents must have made a deal with the devil, because there was no way someone could be so perfect and so evil at the same time.

As I was unable to speak, from rage, I assured myself, not the flush of desire, he continued, "First my class, now the same building. I guess we'll be seeing each other a lot."

I was right, I was in hell.

He made a point of scanning my body up and down, which didn't help the tingling sensation I had going on. My breath caught in my throat. What the hell was happening to me?

"I've got to say," he kept going, "in a purely platonic way, I dig the librarian thing you do normally, but this hobo vibe you've got going works, too."

Rage burned away any remnants from whatever stroke I was having. Dash. Desire. Honestly, maybe I shouldn't ever have chocolate again. Clearly it was the devil's work. "Have you ever heard of sexual harassment?" I asked with faux sweetness.

"Trust me, sweet cheeks, no one is harassing you, sexually or otherwise." He walked backwards with that damn smirk and winked at me before turning and saying over his shoulder, "I'll see you Monday in class, Lay."

If I wasn't certain there was a rule against maiming a T.A. I would have beaned him with my cell phone right in the center of his big, fat head. Instead, I dialed and put it up to my ear.

"Code Red," I said. "Can you meet in an hour?"

* * *

"HERE YOU GO," the waitress said, as she placed a big glass of wine in front of me. If I couldn't have chocolate, at least there was wine. "Can I get you ladies anything else?"

Ember smiled and lifted her margarita. "We're good, thanks."

"Put hers on my tab," Charlie added as she gestured to me, then sent me an apologetic look. To me, she said, "It's the least I could do."

Damn right. She owed me a lifetime of wine to make up for this egregious lapse in girl code. I took a deep gulp of wine, then another. "It's a good thing I love you because this is a betrayal of the worst kind. If this didn't taste so good, it would be dumped over your head right about now."

Charlie slumped and gestured to the waitress for another round. Ember giggled, then licked the rim of her glass. "You can't blame her," Ember said after a drink. "She's had her hands full with Liam and starting her new job."

Another gulp. "No excuse." I wondered if I could mainline wine. I would have asked Charlie if there were any wine-IV protocols, but she was on my shit list.

As though her urge to apologize overcame her self-flagellation, Charlie burst out, "I'm *sorry*. I'm so sorry. I had gotten off two twelve-hour doubles and could barely keep my eyes open, let alone process what Liam was yammering on about. Especially when he comes to bed without a shirt on, talking about the cute little animals he's been working on." Her eyes went misty and Ember began to fan herself. "You know how I likes it when he is all swoony and half naked."

"*Please*, continue," Ember said, leaning in. "I've been on a six-month hiatus since Chris went back to Miami. I need *any* form of swoony and half-naked I can get."

"Men are scum," I said firmly before Charlie could go off a Liam tangent. It was imperative I didn't let any intrusive thoughts of Dash half-naked or otherwise take root or I'd be like Ember, practically panting again. "I hate them all." There, hate was easy. Hate would abolish the image of Dash naked.

"All?" Charlie asked, after sharing a glance with Ember. "Or just one in particular?"

"Don't give me those looks," I warned them. Their tone had me bristling. "You two may have lucked out, but you're not being stalked by Satan."

Ember grinned over her margarita. "C'mon, Lay, he can't be that bad."

I hung my head. "I was wearing my gym clothes and he called me a hobo." It was easier to focus on insults than the real reason why I was so unsettled by Dash's reappearance. It had been easy to focus on rivalry. This...reaction to him? So much worse.

The two of them snorted and I wondered why I needed

friends at all. Clearly the camaraderie we shared had been tainted by Dash's mere presence.

"This isn't funny! It was one thing when he was the idiot upperclassmen who couldn't stop picking on me, but it's entirely another when he's responsible for my grade. Do you realize what it could mean if I fail his class?" Other patrons began to look in my direction as my voice turned shrill. I lowered it to a whisper-shrieked, "Fail!"

Ember put down her glass and leaned forward. "So what? You don't even *want* to get a degree in business."

It was a discussion they'd had with a me a thousand times, and even though I agreed with them, the maternal guilt was strong. "I've come this far, I might as well finish," I argued. It was the same thing I told myself each night as I slogged through business homework I didn't give a damn about instead of following my passion.

"It's just one class," Charlie reasoned. "You're the smartest person I know. All you have to do is make it through one class."

I drank some more. I was going to be an alcoholic by the time the semester was over. "Let's change the subject. I'll survive living in the same building and being his student—somehow, but for now, I want to forget."

"Sure, he's a pain in the ass, but at least he's nice to look at," Ember said.

"Did you hear me?" I asked. I absolutely, positively did not to think about how nice he was to look at.

"If *I* had his class, I'd sure be doing some looking."

My eyes rounded. "Charlie! What about Liam?"

Charlie laughed into her sangria. "What? *Just* looking."

Slumping back in my seat, I studied my friends as they doubled over with laughter, eyes bright from the alcohol. This was exactly what I needed. So, they hadn't been much help taking my mind off of Dash, but they'd loosened the knots in my stomach—at least until I had to see him again on Monday.

CHAPTER FOUR

DASH

IT DIDN'T ESCAPE my notice that I was teaching a class about ethics and fantasizing about one of my students. There was just something about the way she'd shoot daggers at me when she thought I wasn't looking that did it for me.

When other students would give me coy looks from underneath their lashes or leaned forward to expose their cleavage, Layla snarled insults under her breath and countered every argument I proposed.

She hated me, that was clear. Maybe I loved antagonizing her so much because a part of me hated her, too. Hated that she made me feel, hated that she made me want. And I hated that I didn't hate her the slightest bit.

As I gave my lecture, I attempted to focus on anyone but her. Except, the more I tried to ignore her, the more she invaded my thoughts.

With my mind half on the discussion, my thoughts drifted

to the last time I saw her before my junior year abroad. I'd gone to my younger brother's graduation—they'd been in the same graduating class in high school—and I couldn't resist needling her for being salutatorian instead of valedictorian.

"What is he doing here?" Layla asked my younger brother Brian, who was already smiling. He got off watching Layla's hatred of me. I had to admit, so did I.

It was so out of the ordinary to have a woman who didn't fall at my feet. It was refreshing. Distracting. And it turned me fucking on.

I should have been focused on my upcoming year abroad, but as I strolled over to where Layla and Brian were standing outside of the auditorium, all I could think about was her.

She wore a snug white dress fitted to curves she hadn't possessed two years ago when I went off to college. Pale, milky skin filled my vision and her legs went on for miles, accentuated by heels that brought the top of her head almost to my shoulders. She was even more attractive when she turned to me and scowled. It made me grin as wide as I did the first time she didn't fall at my feet. A scowl from Layla Tate was more enticing than a smile from any other woman.

"Come on, Lay, you didn't think I'd miss the big event, now did you? After all, I've been waiting to see you graduate as vale-dictorian for a long time." Her eyes could have singed me with the force of her glare. "I guess I'll be waiting for a while."

"You're such an asshole." She bared her teeth with the words, her cheeks reddening.

"But you love me," I teased, wondering what it would take to truly push her over the edge.

"I loathe you."

She spun around, her dark, sleek hair fanning out behind her. A part of me was disappointed to watch her leave, but I knew she couldn't stay away for long. Much as I seemed to annoy her, it didn't seem to make stop her from coming back for more.

My brother turned to me, backhanding me on the shoulder. "Dude. Why do you always have to give her such a hard time?"

I threw an arm around his shoulder and tugged him along toward our waiting parents. "She wouldn't put up with me if she didn't like it," I told him.

At least that's what I thought, until I came across her behind the sound booth I'd been asked to manage. She was huddled behind it crying.

"Layla?" I asked before I could think better of it. I didn't know jack shit about handling crying females, let alone one who practically clawed at my throat on a regular basis.

Her red-rimmed eyes shot to mine and her face crumpled when she realized it was me. "What are you doing here? Go away!" Except she could barely speak between sobs.

I knelt down beside her. It was a bad idea, but part of me was concerned I'd made her cry. "Hey," I said, as I scooted closer on my knees. "I didn't mean to make you cry."

Her tears undid me. It was one thing to see her riled up and angry and quite another to see her hurt and vulnerable.

Even though she was crying, she laughed. "As if I'd care

enough to cry over you. Not everything revolves around you. Idiot." She wiped at her nose and kept her eyes downcast.

Bumping shoulders with her, I sat next to her on the floor of the booth. We had some time yet before the ceremony was going to start. I couldn't seem to make myself leave without knowing what had made her cry.

"Then why are you?"

She sniffled, wiping her face with her sleeve again. Her mascara had begun to run, and her porcelain skin was blotchy. "What do you care?"

It hurt me, more than it should, to have her think so terribly of me. For a moment, I wanted to console her. "C'mon, Lay. I should be the only person who gets to pick on you. If someone is infringing on my territory, I want to know so I can kick their ass."

"Oh, please. You're probably loving this." For some reason, that made her cry harder and I panicked.

"Hey, hey. No, I don't. I may be a dick sometimes, but I'm not a monster," I said, except, seeing her cry, it made me sort of feel like one.

"It doesn't matter." She sniffled again, wiped her eyes, then pulled out her phone. At the sight of the time, she squeaked, then opened up the selfie view on her camera to check her face. With a low moan, she began to repair the damage. "You can go now, I'm fine."

My first thought was no, no she's not, but I didn't comment on it. Instead, I said, "Actually, I can't. They needed me to help out with the sound system, the music." When she got up to leave, I blocked her way.

"Don't start," she warned.

"I'm not letting you leave until you tell me why you're so upset."

"It's really none of your business."

"So I'm making it my business."

"Let's not do this right now, Dash. I have to go or I'm going to miss my own graduation."

"Then you'd better get talking, because I'm not letting you out of here until you do."

Her sky-blue eyes lifted and met mine. "If you must know, if you just have to humiliate me one more time on what's supposed to be one of the best days of my life, it's my mother. I didn't make valedictorian like my sister so she's very embarrassed to be seen with me today. There? Does that make you happy?" She laughed, but it was hollow. "Maybe you should go find her, you can make fun of me together."

Knowing if I sympathized with her it'd only make her angrier, I got to my feet and helped her up. The wary look in her eyes told me she didn't trust me for a second. I didn't blame her. She shouldn't.

It may have been the tears, maybe she was right, and I was a twisted prick. It may have been the warning in her eyes. It was certainly the dress and her go-fuck-yourself sneer.

I think she knew what I was planning before I did, because an instant before my lips touched hers, she opened her mouth to *protest. Bad choice on her part because it gave me the perfect opportunity to see if her feisty mouth tasted as good as it looked.*

It didn't. It tasted better.

Later, I'd tell myself it was a one-time thing. Something to distract her from her pain, but it'd be a lie.

She went as still as granite in my arms for a couple long, tension-filled heartbeats and then she melted and gripped my shirt with both fists. I could taste the salt of tears on her full lips, warring with the sweetness of her mouth.

It was so Layla I nearly smiled. The contradiction of soft and steel gripped me so hard I lost my hold on sanity.

Turning, I pinned her against the wall of the sound booth. It was dark enough my other senses were heightened. All I could see, smell, taste, or hear was Layla.

She made a sound of pleasure against my lips that shocked me back to reality. I pulled away, and gave myself a moment to savor the look of pure bliss on her face, before I untwined myself.

"Now you've got something to remember me by," I told her.

It took her a moment for her eyes to refocus. When they did, the anguished glaze was gone. Instead, they lit with fire. That I knew how to handle.

"You son of a bitch," she growled.

I couldn't help the smile. "You don't have to be upset, you liked it."

"Liked it?" Her voice was nearly a screech. "You disgust me," she said through clenched teeth and stalked off."

"You and me both," I said to her retreating back. But she didn't hear me.

At least she wasn't crying anymore.

* * *

I MADE it through the lecture, barely, but I made it a point not to draw Layla's attention. Not when the memories of her mouth were so close to the surface. Antagonizing her was one thing, but going down memory lane was another.

That didn't stop me from watching her as she gathered up her books and strode out the door. I was going to hell for loving that it was still warm enough for her to wear her go-to sundresses. All I could think about through my next class and lunch was how much I wanted to see what she had on under them.

Thursdays were reserved for dinner with my grandfather and the memory of Layla in that form-fitting white dress was all that was going to get me through it.

Edward Hampton was an exacting man with expensive tastes and impossible standards. His expectations of me had been drilled into my every waking moment since I was six. It was a wonder my dad turned out okay, considering who raised him. Dad liked to say it was my mother's softening influence that kept him from turning out like his father.

"You're late," he said without looking up from the papers on his desk.

"Class ran over," I answered. It hadn't, but we both knew that. I didn't want to spend more time with him than necessary. Sad, when you considered he was family. He and my grandmother had been married forty-three years, but you wouldn't know that by looking at them.

I kissed my grandmother on the head, causing her to frown. Physical affection was rarely tolerated. "Sit down, Dashiel."

"Dash," I corrected because I knew it irritated her. They didn't pull this kind of crap with my younger brother, Brian. He wasn't required to attend meals or check in. He flitted around the world under the guise of finding himself and no one batted an eye. No, I was the first born, the legacy for the Hampton name.

Her mouth puckered and she indicated the food already laid out on the table. "Dinner's already cold. If you'd called to say you were going to be late, I could have held it, but you'll have to make do."

"That's fine," I answered and spooned up roast with potatoes, peas, and carrots. Thursdays were practically the only day I got a well-cooked meal, so it didn't matter to me if it was cold. "So, what was so important?" I asked. Grandmother had called that morning to mention no less than three times I couldn't skip.

"Since this is your last year of graduate school and you've sown your oats and procrastinated long enough, it's time you accepted your responsibilities as a Hampton."

It's the same speech I'd gotten every year since I was a child. "I'm not ready," I answered as I had every year.

I was going to elaborate, but grandfather didn't give me the chance. Underneath his fake tan and cosmetic surgery, by a confidential and well-paid plastic surgeon, his color heightened. "Elections begin year after next. You'll participate in my campaign, network, get your name out there. By the time your thirty-five you'll be the next Hampton in office. It's what your father would have wanted."

Scoffing inwardly, I stuffed my face with beef and vegetables to keep from saying all the things I wanted to say out loud. Out of respect for my father, I deferred to his parents, but not by choice.

Sensing the growing hostility, grandmother leaned forward, her watery blue eyes bright with excitement. *Shit.*

"We have the most wonderful girl for you to meet. There's a charity function next week, some auction for the needy we're supporting. You'll meet her there. Her family very nice. The Woodburrow's. Good people. You'll like her."

I nodded because it was easier than arguing. The only person in my life who didn't see me for the stepping stone or the legacy, or the pretty face was Layla.

She hated me, but at least it was honest.

I was already looking forward to our next class with renewed enthusiasm.

CHAPTER FIVE

LAYLA

AS I WAITED for the ancient elevator to creak its way down, I scrolled through Instagram looking for inspiration and stopped when I came to the feed of an artist I'd heard of before, but hadn't paid a whole lot of attention to. Peyton Rhodes. They're portraits, stunning portraits. She painted them in black and white so the only aspect you can see is the pure emotion captured from her subjects.

God, what I wouldn't give to paint like that. I spent more time than I should have looking through per past work. She'd only recently gotten into doing portraits. Her parents had died a couple years ago, and she understandably stuck to landscapes while she worked through her grief. According to an interview, it was love that brought her the wave of inspiration to dive back into portraiture.

I wanted to scoff, but it was undeniable how beautiful her work was. I didn't *not* believe in love, but I also believed in evidence. The only example I had for what a relationship was supposed to be like were my parents. My mother ran roughshod over my father my whole life. Was that love? I didn't think so. I wasn't so sure I wanted to take the leap to figure it out.

It was the perfect time for Tequila Tuesday. I needed the break from work, classes, and the carefully plotted game of chess Dash and I had been playing three days a week. It was exhausting trying to keep up with him all of the time. Exhausting, but I'd started to look forward to it.

Hence the need for tequila. Lots and lots of tequila.

Only two months left.

I climbed into the elevator heading Ember's apartment where we decided to host the get together this week. Ember's twin sisters also stayed with her because instead of overbearing parents like mine, she had a pair who couldn't care less. I wasn't sure which was worse. Her siblings had an afterschool thing, and then a sleepover at her aunts so we'd have the place all to ourselves.

Ember threw open the door at my knock, her cheeks already red against her Irish-white skin. "*Hola!* I'm so glad you're here," she squealed.

"Someone's already been in the tequila," I commented with a grin.

"I lost one last night. I figured I needed it."

Ember was an EMT part time while she studied to become a paramedic. I didn't know how she and Charlie worked in healthcare. Charlie was an R.N. having recently graduated and landed her first full-time job. They spent their days saving lives while I drew pictures. Sometimes it felt like my dreams weren't valuable enough compared to theirs. Their jobs *mattered*. They made a difference. But maybe that was my mom's voice in my head. She'd certainly recited the same spiel time and time again.

"Well, let's not disappoint," I said, as I followed her to the kitchen. "You okay?"

She lifted a shoulder. "It comes and it goes. In the moment, it's just about doing what needs to be done next. It's the hours after, when I'm home doing random, ordinary things where it hits me. Sometimes it's not bad. Like if it's an elderly person who has passed due to relatively natural causes. But it's the kids or the parents that get to me."

I saw her eyes flit to the pictures on the wall of her siblings. "Double for you then," I announced to distract her and set my supplies on the counter. Crossing to the tequila station, I whipped up a quick round. "When is Charlie going to get here?"

"You rang?" Charlie said, as she and her best friend and boyfriend Liam walked through the door after knocking. "Time to get this party started." She was still in her scrubs, her dirty blonde hair in a messy topknot, but her eyes were bright and full of life.

Smiling, I lined up four shot glasses for all of us and opened a new bottle—Ember had apparently finished off the rest from our last Tequila Tuesday. With an efficiency that spoke to exceptional competence at her job, Ember sliced limes and salted rims.

Liam automatically went for the TV remote and put on

some football game. As we readied our shots, he settled into the couch.

"What's Chris doing this weekend?" I asked.

It was a touchy subject. Their on-again-off-again relationship was full of more drama than I could keep up with. But what did I know? I'd barely ever had a boyfriend. Even the thought of bringing someone around made me cringe. Not only would my mother have gone ballistic, I wouldn't know what to do with one if I had one.

Ember rolled her eyes. "No talking about that either. Just drinking."

I couldn't argue with that, but I made a mental note to bring it up later when she wasn't heading toward sloshed and so obviously emotionally raw. I held up my shot glass full to the rim. "What are we toasting?" I asked.

"Knock-knock," interrupted an all too familiar voice.

No.

I almost wished I was hallucinating. It'd be better than the alternative.

I spun around, the tequila sloshing over my fingers, to find Liam letting Tripp and Dash in the front door. He looked so good it made me sick. He'd always looked good, even in high school. Perfect clothes, perfect hair. Expensive watches and a fancy new car when he'd turned sixteen. My mother had provided anything I'd ever wanted, but I never had the knack for labels like Dash. He wore wealth casually, like it was meant for him.

Much as I despised him, maybe it was. He'd changed from

what I'd deemed his professorial look—neatly pressed and expertly fitted khaki pants and a button up shirt rolled at the sleeves and open at the collar—to dark jeans, sneakers so new they were still pristine, and a red t-shirt that fit him like a glove. His green eyes winked and that full, mouth was pulled wide into a knowing smile.

My heart sank. My stomach clenched. I wasn't so sure it was from repulsion, but I'd blame my any residual attraction to him to the tequila. How had I forgotten my friends were chummy with Satan himself? I sent them a furious look, but they only giggled at me. The both of them were convinced there was something more between us aside from complete and utter hatred. No amount of my convincing on girl's night could sway them.

"Are we just letting in anyone off the streets now?" I asked shrilly. Without waiting for their answer, I prepped myself a second shot.

I was going to need it.

"I'm wounded," Dash said and snatched the new shot straight from my hands. "I thought we were getting along so well."

"Oh, I'll wound you all right." I lifted my remaining shot glass and hastily clinked it with Charlie and Ember, who could barely contain themselves. Why I put up with them, I'd never know.

Dash watched with those potent green eyes that haunted my dreams—make that nightmares, I corrected firmly—as I licked the salt from my hand, slung back the shot, then sucked on the lime. I don't know if it was the burning heat from the alcohol, or the flash of something in Dash's eyes, but a wash of pure electricity flooded over me and settled low in my stomach. Good God, did tequila have the same wall-eroding effects that chocolate had? What was going wrong in the world that two of its most delicious substances could fail me so spectacularly?

As the alcohol burned its way down my throat, I coughed and asked, "What are you doing here? Isn't there some sort of rule about fraternizing with students?"

"Hey, we like Dash," Liam interjected.

"Yeah," Tripp added. "He brings the fancy expensive tequila on his nights."

"Sellouts," I muttered. I pointed a finger at Tripp, who sputtered. "See if I bring you donuts to the dugout this year." Tripp played college ball for the university team and was being considered for pro ball. He's had it bad for Ember for years but settled on being her friend when she and Chris hooked up. Why couldn't I have a stalker like Tripp, who was as wholesome and kind as they get? I frowned at him, until Dash shifted and caught my gaze again.

Maybe it's because I'd always had a thing for bad boys. Tripp was nice, maybe a little too safe for me.

While Ember and Charlie were busy making drinks and chatting with Liam and Tripp, Dash ambled closer. "It's not against the code of conduct unless you make a move on me. Then we'd be in some trouble. Why does it matter, Lay?" He leaned onto the counter, his eyes twinkling with mischief. "Thinking about making a move on me?"

"You wish," I hissed. I was comforted to learn he had to keep his distance, but I wasn't sure if it was because I wanted him to—or because I didn't.

"Another!" Ember shouted from across the kitchen, already overcome with giggles. She wouldn't say it, but I knew she was missing Chris. I gave Dash one last scathing look, and then joined my friends.

Dash watched me again, I could practically feel his eyes on me, but I ignored him. Charlie finished prepping mean ass margaritas and we chose a board game from Ember's stash. They were always missing pieces because of the kids, and some were so worn you couldn't see the boards, but normally we were too shit-faced to care.

A couple hours later, I stumbled my way to the bathroom. Bladder emptied, I splashed some water on my flushed face. The room swam around me pleasantly, and despite Dash's constant comments, I was feeling nice and buzzed. I'd regret it tomorrow when I had to get up early for his class, but for the moment I didn't care.

I stepped out into the hall after drying my hands where Dash was waiting for me.

"I'm going to turn you in for stalking," I said. "First class, then the building, now following me to the bathroom. Those are serious red flags, buddy."

He pushed off the wall and I slipped by him, but in my slightly drunken state, I went the wrong way and he cornered me in Ember's laundry room.

"Running from me now?" he asked.

"No," I said stubbornly.

"Looks like it."

"Then maybe you need to have your eyes checked, Dash."

He made a clicking sound with his tongue. "*Mr.* Hampton," he corrected. "We've talked about this."

I snorted. "In your dreams. Besides we're not in class right now."

I tried to move around him, but he blocked me. My hands bounced off his chest and my body brushed against his. Warning signals went off in my head. A touch of panic mixed in with the tequila and arousal. Dammit, I should have known better than to let him corner me.

"You're right. We're not. Stop trying to get away from me," he said, his tone tinged with frustration. "I'm trying to talk to you."

My hands dropped to my side. "Are you dense? I don't want to talk to you."

He rolled his eyes. "You love talking to me. You just hate that you love it and it pisses you off."

My jaw dropped. "The hell I do."

"Want me to prove it?" he asked, stepping closer.

"I don't want you to prove anything," I said, but the fight had gone from my voice.

The tequila had my muscles feeling loose and warm. The way Dash's body heat began mixing and sparking with mine clouded my head, my judgment. I knew I should get away, but his nearness was more intoxicating than any drug.

"That's because you know I'm right."

Struggling to find a clear thought, I pushed my wild curls out of my face. "You forget, Dash, I've kissed you before and I'm fine never doing it again." There, that ought to shut him up. prove it to him.

But he only smiled. "You think you didn't like it?" he asked.

"The only thing I liked about it was when you finally stopped."

Dash chuckled, lifted a finger to trace a hairsbreadth away from touching my lips. "I think you're lying. You *loved it*."

"The only thing it made me feel was anger, much like your presence is doing right now." The words were nearly a whisper because I was fairly panting at how close his body was to mine, how much closer I wanted it to be. It was as though we were composed of two volatile chemicals that reacted to each other when we were in close proximity. Instead of a slow burn, it was an explosion.

"You aren't mad because I kissed you at your graduation," he whispered in my ear, causing me to shiver against the nearness of his body. "You're mad because you *liked* it."

I pushed away from him and whirled around, hoping he couldn't see the frenetic beat of my heart in my throat. The hum of Ember's dryer tumbling filled my ears and created a cocoon of sorts in the small space. I struggled to find the right words. "You're so full of yourself, Dash."

He stepped closer and my ragged breaths snagged in my chest. "I don't think so, Lay. Not about this."

"Don't come any closer," I warned with my hands in front of me. "I'm not asking to take a trip down memory lane."

"Why? Afraid you might like it?"

I gulped down air, suddenly finding it impossible to breathe. "No," was all I could manage.

"No, what?"

I didn't know anymore. I had to keep my hands in fists at my side to abstain from touching him, though it was the only thing I wanted to do. The bastard knew it.

He took a step back, looking like he felt none of the things I did. His expression was serious as he studied me. "That's what I thought." A smile ghosted across his lips. "You should get some water to drink, Lay. You look a little flushed."

He turned and ambled away with his hands in his pockets as I fumed with impotent rage behind him.

CHAPTER SIX

DASH

IT WAS HALF of the way through the semester, but it felt like it would never end. Seeing her every day was torture of the most delicious kind. I could look, but not touch. Talk to, but not taste.

If I had been entertained by the constant battle of wills before, now I was tortured by them.

Cornering her at Ember's had been a mistake. One I'd do my best not to repeat. It had been exhilarating being so close to her. Watching those baby blue eyes light with indignation, then with heat. A part of her wanted me on some level, that much was clear.

I almost wished I could turn back time and make different choices. Having the image of her—heavy-lidded and a little blurry around the edges was driving me crazy—she was driving me crazy. All I could think about was how much I wanted to see her with those walls down and how much I wanted to be the guy who scaled them.

It was wrong on so many levels.

Ninety-nine percent of the time, she hated me. But that one percent when she didn't? It consumed me.

In class, we both pretended like the kiss never happened. We were polite and professional. I lectured, she turned in assignments. It was as though we knew if we crossed that line again, there'd be no going back. I was never much for self-control, especially not when it came to getting something I wanted, and wanting Layla was becoming something I *needed*.

Normally, I despised charity functions. Rich people rubbing elbows with other rich people who pretended like the mutual dick-measuring made a difference in the lives of people who needed genuine help. If I hadn't been in such need of a distraction, I would have avoided the fundraiser Grandmother roped me into like the plague. However, because Layla was occupying my thoughts with increasing regularity, I submitted and resigned myself to a night of boring conversations and expensive, tasteless food.

"Thank you for coming tonight without putting up much of a fuss," Grandmother said, as I escorted her from the dining room to the lounge.

Dinner had been plain chicken with overcooked vegetables, and I was looking forward to washing it down with a drink from the open bar. "You bet," I said distractedly.

"Since you've been in such a great mood, let's go to the Martins now before they leave for the night. I've been meaning to talk to Janine about her volunteer work." Code for she wanted to railroad me into talking to their daughter, Jessica, before I turned tail and ran.

"Why don't I meet you there? Do you want me to get you something to drink?" I compromised.

"White wine," she replied and lifted her hand in greeting.

I booked it for the bar before she could rope me into socializing without any alcohol in my system. This semester was going to turn me into a drinker if I made it to the other side alive.

"Whatever red wine you have and a beer, thanks," I said to the bartender. I'd overdone it on the tequila and was going to limit myself tonight, but that didn't mean I had to listen to the inane chatter without the social lubrication.

As I waited, a woman by the bar caught my eye. She was sitting prettily on a barstool observing the crowd and sipping a white wine. Her eyes on the projection show playing on one wall of the lounge. I glanced over to see what had her so entranced. It was a slideshow with information about the charity—arts for youth or something like that.

Of course it was.

I downed half the beer and ordered another. There was no getting away from her. At first it was amusing to run into her in class, at my apartment, now it was my own personal hell.

The woman at the bar sighed and shook her head and the movement was so reminiscent of Layla, I did a double-take. Studying her more closely, I noted the full-length, siren red dress with an objective sort of appreciation. It was formfitting with a slit up the thigh and cut so it emphasized her slim, elegant frame. She turned back to the bar, and her face was in shadow from the moody lighting the event coordinators had rigged to imitate intimacy and draw attention to the projection.

She was literally driving me insane. Seeing her everywhere when she was actually there was one thing, but imagining she was there was another. I finished the beer and started the second. Maybe I'd give that Jessica Martin a chance—anything would be better than this.

Then, the woman at the bar turned and Layla and I stared at each other in shock.

I didn't know whether to laugh or start chugging my beer, so I did both. "Before you accuse me of stalking you, I'm here at my grandmother's invitation," I said once I finished the second beer. The bartender asked if I'd like another, but I declined and switched to water. The last thing I needed was to be drunk around Layla again.

"Sure, you are," she said, her tone scathing.

"What are *you* doing here?" I asked.

"This fundraiser, such as it is, is for the art institute where I work part-time. We're trying to raise money to benefit the low-income schools, so their programs don't get cut." She gestured to the slideshow on the projector. "Those are some of my students' projects, not that anyone here seems to care."

"I didn't know you volunteered."

"Contrary to what you may think, you don't know everything about me."

And that was where I should leave it. For now, I was her

T.A. and I'd already overstepped. I should wish her a good night, tell her I'd see her next class, and walk away.

But I couldn't.

"How long have you been volunteering?" I asked. I was a predator scenting its prey. All I wanted was to gobble up each thing about her like it was my last meal. I was going to hell.

She gave me a look like she couldn't quite figure out what I was up to, then sighed. "I'm not into doing this whole thing tonight. Can I take a raincheck?"

"Thing?" I asked.

"C'mon, Dash, I'm serious. Not tonight. I'm tired, my feet are killing me. We're not going to reach our goal and I frankly don't want to argue."

"Who said we had to argue?"

"Dash!" came my grandmother's voice came from behind me. "I have someone I'd like you to meet."

Suddenly the charity had gotten a lot more interesting and it wasn't because of Jessica Martin.

"You should go," Layla said and gestured to the bartender for another drink.

I started to argue, but my grandmother came up behind me and put a proprietary hand on my shoulder. "Dash? I've been calling you. The Martin's are waiting." She noticed Layla drinking deeply from her glass and her lip curled. "Who's this?"

"Layla, this is my grandmother, Elizabeth. Layla is affiliated with the organization. She's a tutor and also one of my students."

Ever one to observe social niceties, she takes Layla's hand.

"A pleasure to meet you. Why don't you join us? I'm sure the Martin's would love to meet you and talk about the organization."

"Of course," Layla said, but her smile didn't quite reach her eyes.

I knew she wouldn't take my offer to bow out gracefully, so I didn't try. Instead, I followed the two of them back to the table where Jessica and her parents sat with my grandfather.

"Neil, Laura, this is Layla, I'm sorry, I didn't get your last name," Grandmother said.

"Layla Tate."

Grandmother scenting blood in the water laid a hand on Layla's arm as they took a seat at the table. "You're not Magdalene Tate's daughter, are you?"

"Afraid so," Layla said with a tight smile, reminding me of how I'd found her at her graduation. Because of her mother.

"So wonderful to meet you!" Jessica Martin interjected. Jessica was everything I could have hoped for in a political marriage (if I wanted one) and my grandmother knew it. She was beautiful, charming, elegant, and poised. In fact, she reminded me of a shark, and she was looking at me like I was a tasty baby seal.

My grandparents and Jessica's family began firing questions at Layla about the charity and her involvement. Unfazed, or perhaps bolstered by the topic of conversation, Layla answered them which gave me time to study her. I could make a career out of looking at her. I'm not sure I'd ever get tired of it.

From my seat next to Jessica, I got an unobstructed view

across the table where Layla was seated by my grandfather, who seemed to be as enamored as I was. At least that was one thing we had in common.

As the two of them began their own tangent about the charity, Jessica leaned down to murmur in my ear, "Your friend seems nice. Are the two of you together?"

"No," I answered and sipped my beer. "She's a student in one of the classes I T.A. for."

"A student, hmm? Then you're single?"

"Why do you ask?" We both knew the answer to that question, but I was enjoying the way Layla was glaring at me with Jessica so close. Sue me. She'd been driving me mad the past couple of weeks. The fucked-up part of me was reveling in the chance to do the same to her in return. That almost encounter in the laundry room hadn't been near enough.

As though she knew what I was up to, Layla intentionally turned her attention back to my grandfather. That didn't stop me from catching her gaze when it wandered back to me from time to time. I didn't discourage Jessica from cultivating an intimate conversation, but I didn't discourage it either. I'd let her down gently at the end of the night.

I'd been with women like Jessica before, and as beautiful as they were, they only wanted me for my face or my name. Neither of which had anything whatsoever to do with me as a person. Ironically, they had that in common with my grandparents. According to them, all I needed to succeed in life were my looks and reputation.

All I needed to be reminded those two things had no real

bearing outside of their rich circles was to look into Layla's eyes and know there was someone out there who saw the real me. Maybe she didn't fall to my feet, but at least it was honest.

It's that thought that has me following her when the evening concluded, and my grandparents were distracted by the Martins and saying their goodnights. I excused myself and followed her to the empty hall outside the ballroom.

"Layla," I said, but she quickened her pace. Damn if I didn't love chasing her. It made me wonder if she liked it as much when I caught her.

"Go back to your family, Dash. It's been a long night and I don't want to fight with you," she said when I did just that.

"Who said I wanted to fight?"

Her hair had started to fall down around her shoulders. Now that there wasn't a crowd around, I let my eyes wander over the deep neckline of her dress and the exposed tops of her breasts. There was just enough creamy flesh exposed to be enticing without being downright X-rated.

"You always want to fight," she said.

"Maybe because you always seem so happy to do it. You especially like arguing with me in class, but that's not what I'm interested in now. Are you okay? You seemed upset."

"You don't have to pretend to be interested." Her shoulders slumped.

"If I wasn't interested, I wouldn't be asking," I replied.

"Fine, but only because I hope my tedious problems will annoy you." She closed her eyes and slumped against the wall. "This benefit was supposed to raise money for low-income schools to support their art programs. I suppose these days, most people seem to t think art education isn't relevant so they're slowly being defunded. We worked so hard with the kids to make their projects for auction and we didn't even make a dent in our goal. Sometimes, when things like this happen, I wonder if maybe my mom is right about art being useless."

"Hey," I said, and leaned next to her. "It isn't useless. The work you're doing matters." She scoffed and I nudged her with my shoulder. "I may joke a lot, but I mean it. Whatever I end up doing with my life won't mean half as much as the time you put in with those kids."

"But my mom—"

"Screw your mom," I cut in and made her laugh.

The moment lengthened, and I became aware of how close we were standing. I turned to face her, studying the genuine smile resting on her lips. I knew I should walk away, but she never looked more beautiful than she did right then.

She had a second of comprehension where her eyes widened, and she brought her arms to my chest before my mouth closed over hers.

CHAPTER SEVEN

LAYLA

HIS LIPS HOVERED over mine like a suggestion and his tongue snuck in like a secret. Dash Hampton was dangerous, lethal even, because one taste made you think the whole ordeal was your idea.

I was being seduced.

I hadn't prepared for it, couldn't protect myself against it. The marginal defenses I had specifically for Dash crumpled as he hooked my chin with his fingers and glued the front of his body to mine.

There was no excuse for it.

No reason.

No plan.

But I melted against him, the heat between us exploding like fireworks on the Fourth of July, and I was powerless against the assault.

I hadn't planned on any of this, certainly not how I

responded to him. Not the way I moaned against his full, soft lips or licked at his tongue. My own shameless response would have shocked me on any other occasion, but there simply wasn't a chance. We went from arguing, something we always seemed to do, to kissing with no pause in between.

I pulled away long enough to suck in a steamy breath. "We have to stop," I whispered. The voice inside my head screamed NO, but I could hear the doors to the lounge open and fill with people as the crowd began to spill out into the hallway.

We were going to get caught. Someone affiliated with the school would see, and we'd both be in deep trouble.

Deprived of my mouth, Dash licked and nibbled down my throat to the neckline of my dress. "This spot right here," he paused with his mouth hovering over the swells of my breasts, "this spot has been driving me crazy all night."

I fisted his hair, my body trembling with a mix of nerves and fear. The combination was intoxicating. Something came over me, something dirty and dangerous. Something I'd never felt in all my life at playing it safe, at being the good girl who never crossed the lines.

Freeing one hand from his hair, I tugged at the neckline of the dress, baring the thin silk bra and my pebbling nipple to his gaze. He licked his lips, his breath shuddering out and bathing my fevered skin. His eyes met mine as he lifted a hand to cup and shape my breast and the connection sent sparks of pleasure along my nerve endings.

My eyes began to shutter closed as he peeled back the material of my bra. I felt the quick lash of his tongue against my nipple, then he was reaching up and cupping my head.

"Watch," he said, his voice harsh and low in the relative quiet. When I didn't immediately open my eyes at his command, his hot, wet mouth closed over the peak and his teeth nipped in warning.

I hissed out a breath and my eyes shot open. Seeing him with his mouth on me, feeling his tongue flicking against the bud of my nipple and watching as he sucked and bit, had all the tender muscles inside of me clenching in sweet agony.

At my moan, he surged up and met my mouth again, his hand going to my breast to tease and taunt. For the first time in my life, I didn't think. My brain simply shut off, like he flipped a switch I didn't even know existed.

"Let's go back to my place," he said against my lips. "Hell, your place, I don't fuckin' care. I want you under me in a bed." His fingers worked quickly, baring my other breast and flicking the peak into a hard point. "Any bed. Mine, yours. Whichever one is closer."

"What about—"

"I don't give a damn about anything else. It's just you and me."

He kissed me again and I had never realized it could be so distracting. That's why it took a few long, heated moments for what he said to penetrate. I pressed my hands to his chest and after a moment, he let me free, though we were both struggling to breathe.

"I can't," I said between panting breaths. "We shouldn't."

His lips moved to my ear. "We can and we should. Fuck everything else. Be with me."

"You don't even like me," I tried to reason.

Dash's chuckle was dark and made me shiver against him. His fingers tweaked both nipples and he pressed me tighter against the wall. I could feel him hard and ready against my stomach. My fingers itched to reach down, take him into my hands and explore.

"You want me to tell you what I like?" he asked. His hands lifted and weighed the tender heaviness. "New on my list are these, but I have a feeling they're gonna rocket right to the top." He brought his thumb to my mouth, slipping it between my lips until I tasted the salt of his skin. "This. This mouth, the way it likes to spit fire sometimes, I love that. But I also like when it's sweet. You're a contradiction, sweet cheeks, and I'm finding I like both sides of you." His lips come back to mine and he bites down, just hard enough to have me gasp. "The sass," he said, then licked and soothed. "And the sweet."

I had to admit, I wanted nothing more than to do exactly as he suggested. Nothing else seemed to matter once he got his hands on me, not common sense, not our past, not the future.

It was exactly that lack of steadiness that had me pulling away. "Wait," I said. "Wait a second."

To his credit, he groaned, pressing his mouth to my neck as he soothed with his hands over my back. Then, he fixed my bra, adjusted my dress—though he took his time about it —and I was half delirious by the time he was done.

As the waves of lust cleared, I could hear the low murmur of people not even a few feet away. My cheeks began to burn with shame and surprise. I'd never done anything like it in my life before. Let alone with Dash, who I'd hated for as long as I could remember.

His eyes met mine and were like burning coals in the dark. There was no hate in them, only lust. "Don't," he said before I could start rationalizing everything away. "C'mon, I'll take you home." He began to move with my hand tight in his, then stopped, his lips quirking up. Then he moved back, tugged the clip that kept my hair up in a sleek bun and watched appreciatively as it tumbled over my shoulders. "That's better."

Without giving me time to think, he pulled me forward and I followed because my thoughts were too muddled to make any sense of what had happened. For the moment, I'd do as he said and not think about it. Tomorrow, everything would turn to normal, but for now, I let him lead.

I waited by the exit, letting to cool evening air wash over my heated skin as Dash left to find his grandparents and wish them goodnight. Keeping my mind carefully blank, I closed my eyes and steeped in the delicious thrum I still felt all over my body.

Was this what people talked about when they spoke of desire? Lust?

I'd dated around, but I'd never really been so attracted to someone that I forgot everything that mattered. Rather than frighten me, it intrigued me. The forbidden aspect excited me. The way he frustrated me now fed into the fire. Would I ever be able to look at him again without remembering the way his mouth felt on me when we were surrounded by shadows and overwhelmed by need?

Another time, I'd agonize over separating the hate from the heat, but as soon as Dash walked around the corner, his hands tucked into the pockets of his tux, his hair still mussed from my fingers, all doubts fled. Except for one.

Was I making a mistake not taking him up on his offer?

"Ready to go?" he asked as he looped an arm around my waist.

For the first time in my whole life, I didn't want to shove him away. Torn, I could only let him lead me around the hotel where the fundraiser had been held, to the parking lot and his car.

He opened the car door for me, shocking me for the second time that night. I folded myself in and the scent of leather and smoke and something citrus enveloped me. It was like being steeped in him, and I wondered if it was soaking into my pores. If it was, would I ever be able to get it out?

Not knowing what to do with myself, how to act now that things had changed, I kept my hands in my lap and my eyes forward. Dash didn't seem to have the same problem. He reached across and gripped my thigh, leaving his hand there like a brand. When he did, I shifted and finally let my hands flutter down to grip his.

Holding onto him that way kept me from focusing too much on how crazy it was. This was Dash! Not only was he the guy who'd spent the majority of our lives torturing me, but he was also the T.A. for the one class I needed to graduate. But there were other reasons why we couldn't be together.

Reasons I never thought I'd tell him...ever.

And I'm not sure if I could.

Despite the muddled state of my thoughts, I relaxed in his car until we pulled up into our parking garage. As he pulled his briefcase from the back of his car, I slipped out of my high heels. I didn't often go for appearance over comfort and when I did, I was always grateful for the time when I could peel myself out of the clothes and shoes and get back into regular clothes.

We walked to the door in silence, and the tension began to build again inside me. This time it wasn't the fun sort clouded by lust. I stopped him at my door with a quick turn and a hand on his arm.

"Wait," I began, but he cut me off.

"No need to give me an excuse. But this is something we'll need to talk about, eventually. It's not a bell we can unring."

"Why not?" I asked.

"Because every time I look at you, all I'm going to be thinking about is how good you taste."

I nearly swallowed my own tongue. "Dash, there's something you need to know."

He lifted a hand. "I don't care about anything that happened before. If you wanna argue with me, I'm fine with that. I like getting you all riled up, but there's more here than that now, and I think you know it."

"That's not it," I said. My heart leapt in my chest. If his kiss hadn't killed me, the nerves might.

"If it's that I'm your T.A. and the rules, then we'll figure that out if it comes to it. You know I sure as hell wouldn't show you any favoritism."

"It's not that, though it does pose its own set of problems."

"Then, what is it?" he asked.

I paused, unsure if I could trust him with such a secret part of me when I hadn't with anyone else. Maybe it was because he'd always treated me without holding anything back. That he pushed me out of my comfort zones that made me say it.

Because it was the biggest comfort zone I had left, and it was now or never.

"I'm a virgin," I said.

CHAPTER EIGHT

DASH

"A VIRGIN," I repeated.

Layla's cheeks burned bright red, but I didn't think it was because she was still turned on.

"That's right," she said. In a move that was entirely Layla, she didn't look away in embarrassment. That color rode high in her cheeks and her eyes were bright with emotion, but she held my gaze as I rolled the new information around in my head.

I settled on, "Thank you for telling me," when I could get my brain and mouth to make a meaningful connection again.

Her lips trembled with humor. "You're welcome?"

I scrubbed a hand through my hair and laughed. "You gotta give me a minute to wrap my head around this."

She shrugged. "There's nothing to wrap your head around. Tonight was a mistake." Turning, she unlocked her door, trying to play it cool, but I didn't miss the way her fingers trembled around the keys.

"Can I come in?" I asked quietly. "I think we should talk."

"There's nothing we need to talk about."

"Bullshit," I replied.

"I don't think so. It was a mistake. Nothing good could come from taking this any further."

"If you truly believe that, then stop me from coming inside."

With my eyes on hers, I reached past her and pushed open her front door. Her arms fell limply to her side. Tension rolled off her in waves, but she didn't stop me as I moved around her and into her apartment.

I knew I shouldn't be there. If I had any sense of self-preservation at all, I'd turn around, tell her we'd keep our relationship strictly professional—aside from the occasional exchange of insults—and never see her again unless it was in a crowded room.

But I didn't.

Instead, I ventured father into her apartment. Unlike Ember's cluttered chaos, Layla's place was tidy. A small cream sectional framed the living space, draped with a soft, blue blanket and emerald throw pillows—the kind of shit I'd never think to put in my own apartment. Other jewel toned accents throughout the room made the place homey and attractive. It's must have been her artist's eye that gave her such a knack for color.

I took a seat on the couch and faced Layla, who'd closed the door behind her, but hadn't come any closer. Patting the spot on the couch next to me, I said, "Come here."

She hesitated, her arms crossed around her waist, then joined me, sitting stiffly, but her eyes were on me, which I took as a positive sign.

"Do you want me to resign?" I asked before she could clam up any more than she already had.

Layla's eyes shot to mine. "No!" she exclaimed. "Of course not."

"If it's the conflict of interest you're worried about, I'll figure something out."

"I'd never ask you to do something like that, Dash."

"Then, what is it? Talk to me, sweet cheeks."

The name had her mouth tightening with anger, like I knew it would. I'd much rather have her spitting fire at me than clamming up like she was.

"I don't want you to think of me like a conquest. Just because I'm the only woman who's ever said no to you, doesn't mean I'm going to let you get in my pants so easily."

I nodded. "That's fair. I haven't exactly been the nicest guy in the world to you, but that doesn't mean I'm a complete asshole." She gave me a look and I amended, "Well, not in this situation. C'mon, Lay, give me a break." When she retreated into silence, I said, "Never, though, really?"

I couldn't wrap my head around it. Layla was beautiful, maybe not the smoldering sexuality like Jessica, but she had a quiet, unassuming beauty that you may overlook the first time, but that hit you like a freight train the longer you studied her. But it was more than her looks. She had to have had guys flocking after her. I'd seen enough of them panting after her to know that for sure.

"Really."

"Not that it's any of my business, but why?"

She lifted a shoulder. "Just never seemed like the right time or the right guy and I didn't want to have sex with someone just to say I did. Call me crazy, but I wanted it to mean something, at least the first time. Sorry if that ruined your plans."

God, she slayed me.

I moved closer to her on the couch and she stiffened at my nearness. Tucking a lock of her hair behind her ear, I said, "You didn't ruin anything. I'm just not sure where you want me to go from here."

"You're not upset?"

"Of course not." I relaxed back against the couch. "I didn't kiss you because I wanted to sleep with you, well, it wasn't the only reason. I kissed you because I wanted to. I've been wanting to do it again for a long time."

She nibbled on one of her nails and adjusted her legs so one was underneath her body, the other dangling off the edge of the couch. "You have?"

Groaning, I closed my eyes and recalled exactly how she tasted, how she felt. "You have no idea."

I heard the shuffle of fabric rustling, then felt the couch shift beneath Layla's weight as she moved closer. "Could I—would you mind if I touched you?" she asked with such plaintive innocence, I groaned.

"I'm not sure if you should," I said with brutal honesty.

When I opened my eyes she was sitting so close I could smell the remnants of her perfume and feel the flutter of her breath against my skin. Maybe coming to her place wasn't such a good idea. We're alone here. No interruptions. It would be so easy to convince her to succumb to me.

But I didn't want that.

I wanted her to be with me of her own volition.

"Why not?" she asked.

"It's one thing to be with me, it's another for it to be your first time. I'm—" the words tangled up in my chest. "I'm not sure I'm a good enough guy for you to share that with."

The tension around her eyes and mouth softened and a little smile tugged at her lips. "You can't be serious."

"Dead serious, sweet cheeks."

The use of the nickname didn't distract her like I'd intended. Instead she shifted closer. I fisted my hands into the couch cushions so I wouldn't reach for her.

"Does that mean if I won't have sex with you tonight, we can't do anything else?" she asked solemnly.

"I think we've done enough for now."

"Then why did you come inside?" She'd moved closer and her lips were at my ear. I shivered and she nuzzled against the skin there.

When I spoke, it was through gritted teeth. "Because I wanted to make sure you were okay."

"I said I was a virgin, Dash, not that I was completely inexperienced."

With that statement, Layla straddled me in one swift movement that had my eyes popping open and my hands settling on her hips. "What are you doing?"

She fitted her mouth to my neck, and I arched back, but there was nowhere to go. "You're crazy if you think you aren't good enough for anyone," she said against my skin.

Sweet mother of God, I could feel the heat of her through my jeans and the strain of my dick against my zipper was going to send me to an early grave. "That's a veritable compliment coming from you."

"I'm pretty sure it *was* a compliment." Her fingers began mapping my shoulders, tracing my chest, and I wondered if I was in heaven or hell.

"I always knew you were sadistic," I managed to say.

She let out a throaty giggle. "I think you're masochistic because you sure seem to like it."

My hands bit into her hips. "Oh, I like it, but you need to stop."

Layla ground down onto my erection. "Are you sure?"

"Christ, Layla," I bit out, then drove my fingers into her hair. I took her mouth with a violence that shocked the both of us. After a few moments, I broke it off. Breathing hard, I asked, "What do you want from me?" I wanted to tell her, take it, you can have whatever you want, but I didn't think she was ready for that.

"I think I want you, Dash. I don't understand it. It goes against everything I've believed about us for the past...forever, but you make me feel..." Distracted, she rocked back and forth against me. "You make me feel so good."

There was only so much resisting I could do. I tugged her mouth down to mine. Against her lips, I said, "My pants stay on. That's non-negotiable."

She bit my lip. "Are the non-negotiations up for negotiating?"

"Layla," I warned.

Pulling back, she smiled wickedly. "Fine, I accept your terms."

My exhalation rattled out from my lips. Then I reached up and tugged on the sleeves of her dress. It didn't take much to have them sliding down her shoulders, the red material slithering over her skin, silk against silk. She helped push the dress off her arms and down to her waist.

The strapless bra was a thing of wonder. It cupped and lifted her breasts like an offering. I paused to kiss the gentle curves as she arched her back in submission. Fuck everything else, having her in my arms was worth any sacrifice.

When I took my fill, I reached around to unclasp her bra and the anticipation filled me with a tension that threatened to snap my control. She lifted and splay her hands over my shoulders, letting me take the lead. I flicked the clasp and my eyes were glued to the bra as it tightened temporarily, then released.

With a care I didn't know I possessed, I set the bra aside and feasted my gaze on her bared skin. Her breasts were perfection. They fit in my hands like they were made for me. Her pretty pink-brown nipples tightened in my palms as I cupped her. Her head fell back, her hair dangling in a dark curtain and brushing against my legs. With her neck vulnerable to me, I brushed kisses along the expanse of her skin.

"You're so goddamn beautiful," I whispered against her throat where I felt her purr.

"When your hands are on me, I feel beautiful. I feel—"

Her words cut off as I tweaked one of her nipples with my fingers. The strangled cry had me gripping her more tightly.

"What do you feel?" I asked as she trembled.

"Dirty, but in a good way. You make me want to do things."

It was getting harder to breathe. "What kind of things?" I almost couldn't believe I was here, with her half-naked and spread for me on my lap. I didn't know what I'd done to deserve it, but I wouldn't let it go to waste.

"Everything," she said on a sigh.

I groaned and took her with me as I leaned back against the couch. "Stand up," I said with a tap on her ass. "Let's get you out of that dress."

She shook, either from nerves or excitement as I helped her to her feet. Her movements were jerky and hurried while she shoved the dress the rest of the way down. Inch by inch she revealed more of her body and it was enough to make a grown man beg. Soft, soft skin. Sweetly flared hips and shapely legs. A flimsy excuse for panties that made my mouth water in anticipation.

When she stood before me in just those panties and shifted from foot to foot, I reached for her and gave myself a few long moments to run my hands over her. Beneath them, her muscles quivered, and I pressed open-mouthed kisses to her belly and on each hip bone.

She breathed my name like a prayer and I'd gladly go to hell to have the taste of her on my tongue.

CHAPTER NINE

LAYLA

CONTROL WAS a thing of the past.

There wasn't any room for self-doubt.

All I had was the kaleidoscope of sensations inspired by Dash's touch.

At his urging, I stepped forward, but he didn't pull me back onto his lap, like I expected, instead, he tapped my thigh and slithered down until I was straddling his face instead.

"Dash! W-what are you doing?" Stammering, face on fire, I tried to move, but his grip on my thighs was absolute.

He kissed my inner thigh and wrapped his arms around my legs. "I told you my pants had to stay on, but I didn't say anything about yours."

With his eyes locked on mine, he pulled the crotch of my panties aside, then brushed his fingers over me ever so lightly. My knees buckled, but he didn't seem to mind. In fact, he pulled me closer, replacing his fingers with his mouth.

I cried out, unable to stop myself. His tongue slicked over my clit and I gasped in shock. My whole body clenched at the warm, wet sensation.

Dash pulled away, used his fingers to spread me to his gaze. "You said you were inexperienced, but have you ever done this before?" When I didn't answer immediately, he latched on to the enflamed flesh of my clit and sucked.

"T-this?" I asked.

"Mmhmm." I could feel the vibrations of it throughout my whole body.

"No. No, I've never done this."

Somehow, I knew it wouldn't have been as good with anyone else.

"Never?"

"N-no."

"I'll make it good for you." His tongue was apparently good at things other than slinging insults because he was true to his word.

He shifted, adjusted my hips and his tongue slipped inside me and I didn't have the words to tell him so, I only had thin, soft cries of pleasure.

It was a tease, I knew that much. I'd never wanted to be filled so badly in my life. At the same time, I'd never been so wracked with ecstasy either.

Even more than the swipe of his tongue and the pressure of his fingers, as he began his assault against my clit, was the *sounds* he made. It had never occurred to me that a man would make such sounds while he was going down on a woman. He moaned, he hummed. It sounded like he was enjoying the best meal of his life—and maybe he was.

That, along with everything else, is what worked me over the edge. When I attempted to move backwards, away from the constant stimulation, he clamped his hands on my thighs and licked harder, faster. The orgasm locked my muscles tight and I fisted his hands, needing the anchor.

Unbidden, my hips rocked against his face and his tongue slicked back and forth from pussy to clit and then back again. I didn't know I could be so blatantly sexual. I never had been before, but I couldn't seem to help myself.

When I began to shake, Dash carefully rearranged my panties, and then held me steady while he shifted so we were laying on our sides on the couch. He took the throw I'd draped over the sofa back, and shook it out over both of us while I shuddered beside him.

Swamped with an emotional response I hadn't anticipated, all I could do was bury my face in his throat and try to fight my way back to a tentative equilibrium. My breathing erratic, I struggled to get myself under control, but it was almost impossible.

Dash tipped my chin up and pressed a soft kiss to my lips. It was a tenderness I hadn't expected from him, one that undid me as much as any orgasm ever could. I could taste the remnants of my release on his lips and I deepened the kiss, unable to contain myself. Lifting my leg, I wrapped it around his waist, but he made chiding sounds and kept me from grinding against him.

"You okay?" he asked.

Self-conscious now, I nodded, not meeting his eyes.

"Don't be shy now, sweet cheeks. That was the sexist thing I've ever seen. Do you always come that hard?"

I shook my head. "No, nowhere near anything like that."

His hand clenched on my ass where he'd been rubbing to soothe me. "Really?"

"You sound surprised," I said dryly. I hoped the easy banter would help turn things back to normal.

"Nah, I just like hearing how much you liked it."

"As if your ego needed any help."

"That's not why I like hearing it."

The closeness was getting to me. I'd already come once, but I wanted more. I guess that's what people meant when they said once you got a taste, you couldn't get enough. It didn't help that I could feel the hard ridge of his dick between my legs and the aftershocks still coursed through my body.

Trying to focus on the conversation, I squeezed my eyes shut, but that didn't help. It only intensified the sensations. "Why do you?"

His hand trailed up and down my back. "I like knowing I make you feel good."

"Such a change from pissing me off," I commented. I hadn't known it could be like this. Not only because Dash and I were normally at each others throats, but because I'd never been able to relax so fully with another man before. Especially not when I was practically naked, and he was still fully dressed. "Are you sure you won't reconsider the pants?"

"Layla," he said in a warning voice.

"I don't—we don't have to have sex, but I want to see you. I want to taste you and make you feel good, too."

And I did, more than anything. I wanted to satisfy my own curiosity, but I wanted to see him unravel, too. The thought of Dash vulnerable and crazy because of me was more than slightly appealing.

"That's not a good idea," he said, but I could feel his chest rise and fall as his breathing accelerated.

Curious, I made enough room between us so I could slip a hand underneath his shirt. Like a shot, his moved to stop me, but I *tsked*. "You said I couldn't take your pants off. You didn't say anything about your shirt."

He let me unbutton the shirt, slip it over his arms, then throw it behind me, but his expression was stormy. "What do you want to do?" he asked.

His skin was tawny and lightly dusted with springy hair that tickled my palms as I explored his chest. Experimentally, I leaned forward and dragged my nipples across his chest, feeling his warm skin against my own. We both moaned in tandem A his hands fisted in my hair and he yanked me forward.

I could get lost in him, I decided as we battled for control of the kiss. It was bruising, punishing, and I couldn't get enough of feeling the rough contrast of hair against the hard tips of my breasts.

"Hmm?" he prompted. His hand dipped between us to find me wet. I mewled in the back of my throat. "You want to come again? Is my girl greedy?"

I gripped his shoulders with both hands, tried, and failed, to focus. "No, Dash, wait." My protests were feeble at best and he knew it, but I wanted him more than I wanted another orgasm.

My hands dove for the clasp on his slacks. I managed to get it undone and unzipped before he could knock my hands away. I took his mouth with my own and had my hand inside his briefs when he cuffed my wrist with his grip.

"What did I say?" he asked darkly.

I couldn't help but grin. "You said they couldn't come off." He was thick and hard in my hands. I stroked once, slowly, and reveled in his groan. "They're not off."

Silence filled the room, broken only by harsh exhalations, soft groans, or the wet, sloppy sounds of his fingers on my pussy or my hand around his cock. I was seconds away from asking—or begging—to fill me up when he brushed my hands away.

"Dash," I started, but then he adjusted my legs and rolled me to my back. I gasped and then parted my knees for him to brace himself above me. "Oh, God," I said thickly.

"This what you wanted?" I didn't have words, so I nodded. "Stay very still," he warned.

I couldn't have moved if I wanted to, not when he pressed the head of his cock to my entrance and rubbed, torturously, back and forth to coat it with my wetness. One flex of my hips and I could have him inside me. I considered it, but he was thick and long and I wasn't even sure how he'd fit.

Then, he shifted my legs to wrap around his waist and began to rub his cock over my clit with long, slow strokes that sent waves of heat all over me. I reached down to feel him, and he groaned as I cupped my hand over his length to press him harder against my clit.

The head of his cock bumped against my palm with each thrust and he began to groan, softly at first, and then deep and long. Distracted, and rapidly becoming obsessed with the sounds of him in ecstasy, I scrabbled for purchase when he moved abruptly, and his head disappeared between my legs.

This time, he allowed no patient buildup. His tongue honed in on my clit with expert precision, and I gasped as his fingers explored my entrance. As the orgasm swelled, then crested, he slipped in one finger. The burn made me suck in a breath, but any twinges of pain were drowned out as another orgasm swept me away.

When I came back down, it was to the vision of him looking up at me from between my legs, his hand swiping at the moisture on his mouth. Without giving him time to protest, I pushed him back until he was splayed on the couch.

This time he didn't say a word as I tugged his briefs down enough for me to reach in and pull him out. The sight of him had my already tender muscles clenching in appreciation. Dicks weren't theoretically supposed to be beautiful, but his was. A fat, pink head flushed with arousal, slightly thicker in the middle and long enough that I knew I'd feel every single inch.

He let me explore, stroking his length until he threw back his head, his jaw clenched. I knelt between his legs and dipped down for an experimental lick. At his groan, I swirled my tongue around the head, tasting salt and heat. I sucked softly, then took him deep, as far as he could go, and his thighs shook on either side of me.

"Don't take this the wrong way," he said, his voice strained, "but I'm about to come, baby, and you should stop."

Not a chance in hell. If he got to taste me, then I wanted to taste him. I wanted it more than anything in the world at that moment, so instead, I met his eyes, and continued to stroke him. He groaned again, his eyes rolling back. I felt him get impossibly harder in my hands, heard him moan, then tasted his release as he spilled into my mouth almost faster than I could swallow.

When it became too much, he reached down and stilled my hands. I released him with an audible pop, and he gathered me up onto his lap as we both came down.

I wasn't sure where we went from here—where could we?—but I was going to soak up whatever moments we had left until reality came screaming back.

CHAPTER TEN

DASH

WE MUST HAVE FALLEN ASLEEP TANGLED TOGETHER, our clothes half off and me still in my shoes, because when I cracked my eyes open, I found myself in an unfamiliar room with Layla curled on my side, snoring softly. Her hair was a knotted tangle spilling over my chest and her mascara was smeared under her eyes, but she was the most beautiful woman I'd ever seen.

I gave serious thought to waking her up and taking her right there while she was soft and sleepy. I could imagine it, how silky her skin would be under my roughened palms, how her body would wake to my touch. I'd want her on the brink before her eyes ever opened, then I'd want to push her over just as she came fully awake.

One day, maybe, when things weren't so complicated.

Instead, I gently shifted her to the side and brushed her hair away. "Layla." When she only groaned and batted me away, I smiled. "Hey, sweet cheeks, it's time to get up and stop being lazy."

At that, she cracked open a bloodshot eye and glared at me, which—fucked-up as it may be—was almost as satisfying as bringing her to orgasm. She winced and covered her face, then dragged at the blanket covering us to wrap around her body.

As she sat up and stretched, I got to my feet and readjusted my pants, zipped them. I tried not to think about how it had felt to have her hands and mouth wrapped around me, how her eyes had smoldered when she looked up at me with her mouth full of my cock. Tried and failed.

Clearing my throat, I asked, "You mind if I use your bathroom?"

She shook her head, her eyes wide, and I knew she was wrapping her head around what had happened the night before. I wasn't sure what side of the fence she'd land on, but I figured it was best to give her time to adjust. I used the john, washed my hands, and threw some water on my face.

The bathroom is where the scent of her was strongest. From the shower or the perfume bottles and lotions she had on the counter. It made me think of her naked, lathering on soap or spreading cream on her skin, and my dick decided it fucking loved that thought.

I found her in the kitchen wearing a blue silk robe. It was thin enough I could see the material of her thong at the top of her ass showing through. I could get used to seeing her half-dressed and sleep-mussed, I decided, and ambled up behind her. She'd had enough time to adjust and I wasn't going to give her any more to decide it had been a mistake.

She stiffened slightly at my touch as I wrapped my arms around her waist and pressed the growing hardness of my dick against her ass. I didn't want to scare her, but I didn't want her to forget what she did to me either, or what I did to her.

"Dash," she began, then choked on her words when I kissed her neck. Her shiver against me sent shocks throughout my own body.

"Don't get bashful on me now," I said, then moved off to pour us both a mug of coffee. "We're both adults."

She flipped the bacon she was crisping in the skillet. "Yeah, but you're also my T.A. and we could both get into a whole heap of trouble. This...we..."

Handing her mug to her, I tipped up her chin to look into her eyes. "We don't know what this is yet, Layla. I'm not going to push you into anything before you're ready, including a relationship, but most especially sex."

Layla choked on the coffee. "Relationship? *You* have relationships?"

I pressed a hand to my heart. "You wound me again, sweet cheeks. Is sex all you want me for? I feel used."

Fighting a smile, she removed the bacon and put it on a paper towel to drain. "You know what I mean. I've never seen you actually date someone before. I thought you were more..."

"Of a manwhore?" I prompted.

Her cheeks burned and she distracted herself by cracking a

couple eggs into the grease. "No, more casual, I guess. You seemed to like to play the field in high school."

"Maybe that's because the one person I was interested in couldn't seem to stand being around me."

She spun around. "Don't tease. I'm trying to be honest with you."

I shrugged. "Whose teasing?"

Her mouth dropped open and she gaped. "You can't be serious!"

"For someone who claims to be so smart, you sure can be dense sometimes."

At that, she returned her focus back to the food and was silent as she turned the eggs, then plated them with bacon and toast. I allowed her to stew a little, and finished my coffee as I sat on a stool at the little island bar and watched her. Every now and again, she'd glance back as though to reassure herself I was there, then turn back to her cooking.

When she set a plate in front of me, she said, "What do you want from me?"

"To the point then, huh?"

She shrugged. "I don't like playing games. And you're very good at playing them. This is one area where I'd let you win—because I don't like to gamble—and we've both got a lot to lose."

I considered her as I forked some eggs into my mouth. She ate like she did everything else, purposefully, no doubt with a plan and a checklist. As she carefully cut her eggs into neat little sections, I recalled what it had been like to watch her come apart, to taste her release on my tongue, and know she could break apart because of me.

I wanted that again. Wanted to be inside her when she did and feel her grip me tight as she came. I'd be lying if I wasn't hesitant at the thought of being her first, but at the same time, I wanted to take her and make her mine.

"You're talking about the class?" I said when I could speak again.

She nodded, sipped her coffee. "It's a requirement for me to graduate for the business side of my double major. If we got caught, I'm not sure what the consequences are, but the one thing I am sure of is that it wouldn't be pretty—for either of us."

"I get that. You're not wrong to be cautious. I didn't intend for any of this to happen, but that doesn't mean I regret it either."

"Then we're in agreement that whatever this is, stops now," she said primly and bit into a piece of bacon.

I almost laughed and I could hear it in my voice as I said, "Not a chance."

Her eyes bulged. "Dash, as fun as it was, we both could be damaged by the fallout. You could lose your job. My major. Do you really think some orgasms are worth the risk?"

I polished off the rest of my eggs and bacon, then got to my feet and pressed a kiss to her surprised lips. "No, I don't. But I think you are." When she simply stared in shock, I smiled. "I'll see myself out."

Before I could leave, there was a knock at the door. Eyes wide, Layla bolted to press her eye to the peephole. She spun around with a hand pressed to her stomach. Whoever was on the other side, Layla didn't look happy to see them.

Her face drained of color, she said, "It's my mother."

She didn't need to explain for me to understand. I recalled all too well the way her mother had treated her at graduation. And that had only been one slice of one day of Layla's life. Who knew how she'd been treated behind closed doors?

"Get me a ziplock bag full of coffee grounds," I instructed, as her face showed increasing panic.

"What? How can you want coffee right now? If she sees you here, she's going to go ballistic."

"I'll take care of it."

Layla shook her head, but she was too distraught to argue for once. "I don't see how coffee grounds are going to take care of it, but I'm willing to do anything. She can't know about us. Not that I'm ashamed or whatever, but—"

I came up behind her as she measured out coffee. "I'm aware of what your mother is like, Layla. I'm not afraid of her, but if you need more time, I'll give it to you. Now give me a kiss."

Before she could argue, I took her mouth and kissed her breathless, kissed her boneless. When all the tension had eked from her system, I ran my hands up her back, then down to palm her ass. She moaned against my lips and I eased myself away, leaving her breathing heavily.

"That should relax you enough to deal with her, but don't let her bulldoze you over. Pretend she's me," I added with a wicked grin. "You don't seem to have any problem handling me, do you, sweet cheeks?"

She ran a hand through her mussed hair. "I can't seem to figure you out anymore," she said.

"Good, that'll keep you nice and off-balance. Just the way I like you."

Shaking her head, she led me to the door. Bag of coffee in hand, I pulled it open and found Layla's mother on the other side. The look of surprise was worth the entire experience. To Layla, I said, "Thanks for letting me borrow some coffee. I wouldn't have been able to start my day without it. Hi there, Mrs. Tate. Your daughter is a lifesaver."

Blinking owlishly, Mrs. Tate said, "Is she?" with a little wrinkle between her brows that said she didn't quite understand what was going on.

"Nice to see you, ma'am," I told her, then winked at Layla over her shoulder. "Thanks again for the coffee, Ms. Tate."

"Mom?" I heard Layla say as I made my way down the hall to the elevator. "What are you doing here?"

Layla hustled her mother inside, no doubt to keep her from ogling me and putting two and two together. I wasn't as worried.

The look Mrs. Tate had given me was one I well recognized. First there was shock. Her gaze had shifted between Layla and me. From my powers of observation, I deduced she was surprised as hell to find Layla with company over on a weekend, let alone *male* company. When she'd realized who I was in particular, a *Hampton*, her eyes had glazed over with a look I knew all too well.

It was a combination of greed, envy, and appreciation that made me want to duck and cover. No doubt there wasn't much fooling going on as far as why I was in her daughter's apartment, but I didn't want to give her any excuse to make Layla's day harder than it had to be. It probably didn't help too much and I cursed Mrs. Tate for her terrible timing.

All the progress I made was about to be undone, and there wasn't a damn thing I could do about it.

CHAPTER ELEVEN

LAYLA

I WAS at Einstein's the following Monday, trying to pretend like everything was normal. But no amount of cream cheese or cappuccinos could erase the memory of the night with Dash from my mind. And I wasn't sure I wanted it to.

My phone rang and I answered it out of habit, not giving a thought to who could be on the other line.

"What were you doing with Dash Hampton Sunday morning?" my mother asked without preamble. Like she'd been asking ever since she ran into him at my apartment.

So much for carbs cheering me up. I paid the cashier and juggled the paperback with my bagel and the to-go cup of sustenance. "He lives in the building and wanted to borrow some coffee. He'd just moved in. Remember?" If it wasn't in Mom's sphere or directly related to her agenda, it was unlikely she paid any attention to it. I had to tell her two and three times before she remembered anything she didn't consider important.

"I don't think it's a good idea for you to associate with him. His family is influential of course, but he'll just distract you from your schoolwork and the position at Kragen's next summer. Just like your father did with me." No doubt she'd given thought to marrying me off like this was some Victorian era deal to be capitalized on. Her distaste for men after my father left her must have soured her on the thought of the Hampton name.

I pulled the phone away from my ear and wondered if I'd fallen into an alternate universe. Putting it back to my ear, I said, "Who I spend my time with is none of your business. Besides, I can't completely avoid him, he's a T.A. for one of my classes. I literally have to see him three times a week. Not to mention he lives in the same building. I can't use the stairs forever."

Her sigh filled the line. That sigh characterized my child-hood. It said, 'You'll always disappoint me.' "Then drop the class. He's bad news, Layla."

"If I drop the class, I won't have enough credits to graduate with the business degree, Mom, so unless you want me to lose the opportunity at Kragen's, you'll drop it."

Then, I did something I've never done in my whole life, I hung up on her. She called back three times on my way across campus to Dash's class alone, but for once, I wasn't overcome by anxiety because of it. I had bigger things to worry about.

I pushed into the lecture hall and then the nerves made themselves known. How was I supposed to be in the same room with him after what we'd done, let alone along with thirty or so other students?

Dash was waiting at the front of the room, bent over his laptop, a crease between his brows. He wore a thin navy-blue sweater and dark-wash jeans. I'd always known he was attractive, you'd have to be dead not to notice, but now I knew what it was like to feel that body underneath my hands, pressed against my own. It only took looking at him and I was flushed with heat and want.

As though he could sense me, he looked up and I caught him smiling before he smothered it.

Oh, boy, I was in trouble.

"Excuse me," said a petite freshman as she tried to navigate around me.

Ignoring Dash's grin, I took my usual seat in the back of the hall. It used to be because I couldn't stand being so close to Dash for fifty minutes, but now it was because I didn't want to be sitting around any of my classmates while I ogled him and remembered what it felt like when he was hard, hot, and in my hands.

I could barely concentrate as he began his lecture. I was grateful he didn't feel the need to call on me to answer any questions. I couldn't have formed a coherent sentence if I he tried. Besides, I didn't want to draw any attention my way. I was already terrified someone could tell things were different between us even though it had only been one night. *I* felt different. We hadn't even had sex, yet I felt like he was already a part of me, down to my bones.

"Ms. Tate," he called toward the end of class. The way he said my name made my heart flutter.

Then, I smiled a little. Good girl Layla Tate was feeling very bad indeed. "Yes, Mr. Hampton?"

Dash had been leaning across the podium and when his name rolled off my lips, he straightened. There was a lengthy pause and I imagined he was breathing a little harder. I knew exactly how it would sound.

"Can you pass out these assignments for me, please?" I couldn't be imagining the rough edge to his voice, and I could feel his eyes on me as I distributed the papers along the rows of students.

At the end of class, I took my time packing up my stuff and wasn't disappointed when Dash met me at my seat. He leaned over casually, like he was going to talk about the assignment. With heated eyes roaming over me, he said, "I think you need another lesson, Ms. Tate."

I was sure my eyes were sparkling. "Is that so, *Mr. Hampton?*"

"When's your last class?" he asked.

"Cancelled. I'm free the rest of the day. You?"

"Office hours. But I could make myself busy."

I had a feeling I knew how busy he'd like to be. "I'd hate to be the one to interrupt your schedule. Why don't you come over after?"

His smile faded. "Are you sure about that?"

Slinging my backpack over my shoulder, I said, "I guess you'll see when you get there."

* * *

"ARE you sure you know what you're doing?" Ember asked, as I scurried around my apartment wondering how I could accumulate so much clutter in less than twenty-four hours.

"What are you talking about?" I was nearly out of breath from sweeping and scrubbing down counters.

"I saw the way you and Dash were looking at each other when you were at my place. I'm assuming he's who you're cleaning for."

I stopped scrubbing the island countertops. "What are you talking about?"

"C'mon, Layla, I'm not an idiot." She rolled her eyes. "He's your T.A. though. Isn't that like against the rules?"

"Even if something was happening *which it's not*, I'd be careful."

"Layla!" Ember said in a chiding tone. "I'm shocked. I'm all for you losing your v-card, but is Dash really the one you want to lose it to?"

I began to wipe down the counters again, but my mind was preoccupied. It warred between memories of Dash and his near-constant insults throughout school and how it had felt being in his arms.

Ember whistled low and long. "Girl, you don't even have to answer that question. I can practically read it on your face. He must have been a good kisser." My face flamed and split with a wide smile. At that, Ember laughed. "Oh my God, I wish you could see your face right now. He must have done better than kiss you. I want all the dirty details."

I folded over and beat my head against the counter. "Ember, I don't know what I'm doing. Part of me still hates him for, you know, everything he's ever done to me. Trust me, he's been an absolute dick sometimes, but then, I don't know, there's another side to him. One I can't seem to stop thinking about."

"Is that side located in his pants?" Ember asked, her voice colored with laughter.

"Don't joke. This is serious. I don't know what I'm doing."

Ember padded to the kitchen and pulled me upright. Tucking hair behind my ears, she said, "Honestly, Chris and I have been together a long time and sometimes I think I still don't know anything about love or relationships."

"Is something going on? Why didn't you say anything?"

She lifted a shoulder as I went to get her a beer. Screw the house. Dash could wait.

"This long-distance thing is no joke. Sometimes we have to go a couple days without talking now. If I bring up how much I miss talking to him, he berates me for trying to control all of his time. Do you think it's wrong of me to want to talk to him, not all day, but at least once a day? We only get to see each other a couple times a year."

I wish I had the answers for her. I didn't feel nearly well-equipped enough to handle relationship troubles. But she was my friend and she needed an ear. "I think you deserve to get what you want, within reason, from any relationship. To not consider your needs or to belittle them isn't a sign of a healthy relationship. But what do I know."

Ember's smile wobbles. "I don't mean to whine."

Waving that away, I pop the tops to our beer. "Don't even think about it. That's what I'm here for. Why don't I text Charlie and see if her shift is over? We can make it a girl's night tonight instead?"

"You don't have to do that. Even though you're denying it, I know you had some sort of plans tonight."

I already had my phone out to text Charlie and Dash an update. "You come first."

Dash replied almost immediately.

DASH: Still coming over. I don't mind a Netflix and bash man session. I'll bring the wine and chocolate.

Charlie texted a few seconds after that.

CHARLIE: Wish I could! I'm working a double and won't be off for another ten hours. Tell Ember I'll call her tomorrow to bitch after I get off and give her my love. P.S. Chris is a cocksucker.

Ember settled on the couch while I changed from the cute dress I'd put on for Dash into a pair of sweats and a camisole with a shelf-bra. I doubted Dash would actually stay once he realized what he was getting into.

Ember was staring off into space and occasionally sipping from her beer by the time I returned.

"Charlie can't make it, double shift. She said she'd call you after to talk."

Ember smiled wanly. "I'm sorry for interrupting your plans for my pity party."

"Acctuallyy about that..."

I was interrupted by a knock at the door. With a cross between a grimace and a grin, I answered it with a mouthed "I'm sorry" over my shoulder.

Dash stepped in with a bottle of wine in one hand and a plastic bag full to bursting in the other. "I brought supplies." After placing the wine on the coffee table, he added, "I wasn't sure what kind of chocolate this situation called for so I pretty much got one of everything."

Ember's mouth opened and closed. "I've got nothing. What's going on?"

"Layla told me you were having man troubles. I'm here with wine and chocolate and am offering to prostrate myself on behalf of all the male species. Take your vengeance out on me or beseech my wisdom, whichever you choose."

For the first time since she came over, Ember's smile was genuine. She reached forward and glanced through the bag, studied the label on the wine, and then said, "There may be chick movies and crying."

"I'm not afraid of tears and I love me some Sandra Bullock."

Shaking my head at the two of them, I took the bag of treats into the kitchen along with the wine to pour three glasses. When Dash joined me as Ember flipped through Netflix for a movie, I cornered him where we wouldn't be visible from the living room.

"You didn't have to do this," I told him.

He tugged me closer, kissing me firmly on the lips. After a second, I relaxed against him. "I know I didn't. But you can call it shallow if you like. Maybe it's just the way I'm gonna get in your pants for sure."

I rolled my eyes. "Dream on."

As I spooned up the ice cream, he hovered over my shoulder. "Don't tell me rocky road ice cream doesn't make those panties drop."

I glanced up and met his laughing eyes. Slowly, I put the spoon in my mouth and licked off all the sticky sweet goodness. His gaze turned heated and I grinned.

"Take the wine into Ember, will you?" I asked.

He did and shouted, "Time to get white girl wasted!" along the way and I had to put a hand to my chest.

It wasn't the ice cream, but the man, who'd shown me a side of him I hadn't realized existed, that made my panties want to drop.

CHAPTER TWELVE

DASH

"THIS IS the best movie I've ever seen," I said around a handful of popcorn.

Ember rolled her eyes at me, but she no longer looked like a wounded puppy. "You're only saying that because you get to see women prance around in bikinis."

I grinned. "That, too, but seriously. It's got comedy, action, and bikinis. What's not to like?"

Ember eyed me. "Are you patronizing me because I'm being pitiful?"

I tossed a handful of popcorn at Ember, ignoring the "Hey!" of protest from Layla. "Number one, I wouldn't patronize you. Number two, if I hated the movie I'd tell you straight up. Not likely, though as I've always had a thing for Ms. Bullock."

"I don't know why Layla calls you the spawn of the devil. You're not that bad."

"Spawn of the devil?" I said to Layla. "I thought I was God?" I added with an evil smirk.

Her cheeks turned a beautiful rose and I heard Ember choke on a laugh. "On that note, I'd better get going. I've got an early shift tomorrow."

Layla gets to her feet and walks Ember to the door. "You're welcome to come hang out any time."

"I'll bring wine!" I shout.

When Ember leaves, she's got a smile on her face, so I consider my mission accomplished.

Layla gathered the bowls and discarded drinks, shooing me away when I try to help her. "You surprised me tonight," she said as she began to rinse them under the faucet.

"How's that?"

She shrugged. "I didn't figure you for the type who could, I dunno, hang out and cheer up my friend."

"There are a lot of things you don't know about me," I said.

Our eyes caught as she looked back at me. "Will you stay? At least for a few minutes. Let me finish this real quick."

It was a bad idea. She was caught between wanting me and hating me with enough chemistry thrown in to make an already confusing situation even more so. Teasing her, tasting her again was one surefire way to make her virginity go from a sure thing to nonexistent.

I leaned against the counter, watching her as I considered. Water splashed up on her wrists, and her hasty topknot had started to come undone and spilled over her shoulders. I liked her this way, a little roughed up, not quite so put together.

Normally, she was meticulous about her appearance, out of habit no doubt caused by her mother, I'd imagine. I liked it even more when she was all mussed-up because of me.

While she cleaned up, I distracted myself walking through her apartment so I didn't drag her down the hall to her bedroom and strip her down. She hadn't begged me to take her...yet, but my control was on a hair trigger, apparently, so it was best for me to keep those impulses locked up tight.

Layla had covered the exposed brick wall with minimalist reproductions of book pages. I moved closer to examine them. Boring, dry lines from ancient English classics ought to distract me from thoughts of her naked.

Except, the pages weren't lines from sonnets or novels, at least not any old ones. There were passages from Harry Potter, Star Trek scripts, Stephen King, and Dean Koontz books. I stood, slack-jawed and stumped for a few long minutes. Layla wasn't only a bookworm, she was a nerd.

I couldn't say why I found that so endearing, or why it made me want to kiss the hell out of her, but it did.

It also made me to want to explore, to learn more, to find out what other secrets she was hiding behind those pretty eyes of hers.

I should pump the brakes, tell her we should cool it off—at least until the semester was over—and we both weren't in danger of screwing things up. It would kill me to be the reason she tripped up for the first time in her life. She already put too much on her shoulders, much as she tried to hide that, too.

As she finished cleaning up, I found my way back into her

bedroom. The scent of her was even stronger here. It surprised me to find Miss-Nothing-Out-of-Place Tate left her bedspread tangled in a heap. Books were stacked three deep on her night-stand. Her closet doors yawned open with clothes exploding out.

I realized my mistake the second I felt her enter the room behind me. Whirling, my heart began a thunderous staccato in my throat. "Finished?" My voice was a croak, my throat unbear-ably dry.

Layla only seemed amused, if the smile on her lips was anything to go by. "Get lost?" she asked.

I had to shove my hands in my pockets to keep from reaching for her. "No. Being nosy."

Leaning against the door jamb, she glanced around her room. "And you decided to poke around my bedroom? What did you do—look in my underwear drawer?"

Disappointed the thought hadn't occurred to me, I lifted a shoulder and nodded toward the hall. "Why don't we go out and watch another Bullock flick?" Anything to get her away from the temptation of her bed.

I tried to squeeze out beside her, but she put a hand to my chest. The subtle contact had me freezing to the spot, all my muscles contracting. "Layla," I warned.

"You didn't have to stay."

"Let's talk about this in the living room," I suggested.

"We can talk about it here." Without giving me a chance to argue, Layla took my arm and led me to the bed. At my panicked look, she laughed. "Don't worry, I'm not planning on making a move on you."

I didn't know whether I should be amused or relieved. "What do you want to talk about?"

She pushed dark tendrils away from her face. "Don't look so serious. I wanted to thank you for staying, for distracting her the way you did. If you're worried, she won't tell anyone."

"I'm not worried," I told her. She nodded, looking at her lap. "I know you are. You're probably confused as hell."

"You're not wrong there. I think what we're doing is crazy. Maybe it's a good thing Ember interrupted tonight. I'm not sure...I'm not sure I would have been able to stop."

She bit her lip, unable to meet my eyes. I wanted to reach out to her, to touch her, but I knew once I got my hands on her, it'd be a slippery slope. "You having second thoughts?"

"I've been having second thoughts the whole time," she admitted. "You know that."

"That's because you think too much."

At my words, she turned to study me. It used to be that I knew what she was thinking just from looking at her. Now, her eyes are shuttered.

Then she met my gaze. "Would you stay?" The words were so quiet, I almost believed I imagined them. "Just for tonight. Maybe I don't want to think anymore."

* * *

THE NEXT DAY, after a night where we cuddled and fell asleep twined in her bed, Layla found me at my office after class and proceeded to make up for all the kissing I hadn't gotten the night before.

Kissing her was better than screwing any other woman, I was almost sure of it. It wasn't because she was innocent, although there was a certain primal possession I got from knowing I could be the only one to be with her, it was just *Layla*. Her smart mouth was even feistier when it pressed up against mine. She battled me as much with words as she did with her kiss and I ate all of it up.

"I have to get to the library. I'm supposed to be tutoring this afternoon." She was giving me excuses, but made no move to leave my arms.

The door was closed. It wasn't locked and that was a bit like tempting fate, but I couldn't find the resolve to move the couple feet to throw the deadbolt. "Okay, then you should get going," I said.

But she deepened the kiss instead. I let her. Delving into her sweet mouth was a level of bliss I wasn't aware even existed. It was a bliss I wasn't wholly sure I deserved.

I carefully disengaged and kept her at arm's length. "Really, Lay, you should get to the library." The throbbing hard-on in my pants disagreed, but now wasn't the time or place.

"You're right," she agreed, her face flushed. She strode to the mirror on the back of my office door and checked her clothes, her hair. The sight of her mussed shirt and smeared gloss made me ache to see her freshly fucked and rumpled in my bed as she woke up still soft and pliant from sleep.

Christ, maybe I was as big of a dick as she thought I was.

Only a total asshole would take advantage of a woman like Layla. She really was one-of-a-kind. Didn't take my bullcrap, smart as all get out, and underneath her sweet, prim exterior, was dynamite just waiting to be lit. God did I want to fucking light her up.

"Do I look okay?" she asked.

I had to force myself to reply with a sarcastic comment to keep from dragging her off to a closet or something. "No worse than usual."

She took it in stride and rolled her eyes before giving me one last kiss that was all too brief. "I'll talk to you later."

I was still frozen minutes later when Jessica strolled through my door without knocking. At first, I looked up with a smile thinking Layla was coming back, but it faded as Jessica's too expensive perfume filled the small space between us.

In order to get away from the cloying scent—and get a safe distance away—I moved to my chair behind the desk. "Jessica. What can I do for you?"

"Isn't she your student? The one who was at the charity dinner?" She asked it in such a way that I knew she was already aware of the answer. It was a leading question, one designed to catch me in a lie. "I saw her leaving your office."

I studied Jessica in her perfectly pressed jeans and meticulously planned coordinating accessories. She looked like the kind of fake-Instagram ready that made me want to close my head in a door. "What she is or isn't is none of your business."

She chuckled, a deep, throaty sound that would have been sexy if it came from any other woman. "That's where you're mistaken, Dash. I know what I want, and I won't hesitate to go after it. And you're what I want."

"I'm flattered, really, but I'm not interested."

Her eyes flashed in warning. "Because you're fucking your student? That's one way to ruin your candidacy before you've even gotten elected."

Hovering between amused and an insulted, I merely leaned back in my chair. "I'm not interested because of *you*, Jessica. Cold and calculating isn't really my type. Now, if you don't mind, I've got office hours and papers to grade. You can see yourself out."

When she didn't move, I looked back at her. "Is this where you say I'm going to regret this? Because I won't entertain any threats from you."

She smiled, showing off perfect teeth that must have cost a fortune. "Some things don't need to be said. I expect to have an invitation to the gala your grandmother spoke about at the charity function by this weekend, Dash. Give your grandparents my best. Your grandmother has all of the details."

I closed my office door behind her and frowned.

CHAPTER THIRTEEN

LAYLA

"SO, SPILL," Ember urged, her eyes gleeful over the top of her glass. "What's been going on between you two?"

I took a sip of my own, barely tasting it, as I considered my answer. My friends would understand if I chose to continue my —whatever it was—with Dash, but for some reason, I couldn't bring myself to tell them.

"Nothing." At their disbelieving look, I rolled my eyes. "I'm serious! Besides the fact that he's been an absolute douchebag to me for the past however long, he's also my T.A. Even if we were to, hookup or whatever, it would run the risk of us both getting into major shit. You know me better than that." For additional emphasis, I added, "Could you imagine what Mom would say if that happened? I'd be doubly screwed."

"Let me tell you as someone who recently went through this parental bullshit," Charlie began. "Yeah, your parents are important, but you have to realize this is *your* life. You've got to start living it for you. Period."

Ember nodded emphatically.

I pointed to her. "Don't start."

She raised her brows. "What?"

Wanting to change the subject, I gestured with my glass. "Since we're talking about living our lives. What about you?"

Ember sat back in her seat, trying to look innocent. "I don't know what you're talking about."

"Yeah, what's up with Chris?" Charlie asked.

"I thought we were here to figure out the Dash situation."

I made a zipping motion over my lips. "Charlie still hasn't been caught up on everything that happened. Besides, I can handle Dash for now. Even though *nothing* is going on."

"I don't want to talk about Chris," Ember said with a frown. "Talking about him depresses me."

Charlie covered Ember's hand with her own. "That's not a good sign, sweetie. Tell me what happened."

Ember signaled the waitress and ordered another round. With a heavy sigh, she began, "He wants to take a break, which can't mean anything good. He says we need space because it's our senior year and our lives are about to change. I told him I'd support him in whatever he wanted, like I always have, but he said he needed time."

"A break in a relationship is never a good sign. The whole point is to work through problems together," Charlie said wisely.

I had to defer to her limited experience because I had

exactly none. I was in over my head with Dash as it was. The only thing I knew was that Chris was making my friend unhappy and if anyone deserved happiness, it was Ember. The girl was as selfless as it got.

Ember lifted a shoulder. "I want him to be happy. I don't know. Things have felt off for a while. I guess I haven't wanted to see it."

"What are you going to tell him?" I asked, my heart aching for my friend.

She downed her drink. "I want to tell him if he's that uncertain about me and our relationship, then he can pound sand."

Charlie and I clinked our glasses. "I agree," Charlie said. "You want someone who *wants* to be with you, not someone you have to convince."

I studied the liquid in my glass. Charlie had a good point and I couldn't help but think about her words as they applied to Dash.

Was Dash with me because he wanted to be? Or was it because of the thrill or the challenge? It was something I should definitely figure out before things went too far. We were already flirting with the line. I needed to figure out what he wanted from me, but also what I wanted from him. The attention was nice, the way he made me feel was undeniable...worth the risk? I wasn't sure.

"I know. I know," Ember continued, pulling me from my thoughts. "Intellectually, I realize you're right." She thumped her chest with her fist. "It's my heart that needs to catch up."

I knew that struggle well enough. My heart was telling me to go for it...but my head was saying not so fast.

"We only want you to be happy," I told her.

Charlie nibbled on a pretzel. "Are you?" she asked Ember.

"Am I what? Happy?" She paused after Charlie's nod. "Well, in general...I guess not. I mean, I want to finish school to become a paramedic. I'd like to have time to be a regular college student instead of parents to my kid sisters and I'd really love it if my parents would stop being such drunks. With Chris? No. Definitely not. I guess that's my answer, huh?"

Feeling the need to lighten the mood, I said, "I guess now you can let Tripp land one."

Charlie snorted, then choked. She tried and failed to stifle her laughter behind one hand.

Ember blushed prettily and shook her head. "Tripp doesn't see me like that. We're just friends."

"Just friends," Charlie said with a knowing smirk. "That's what I used to say about Liam and now look at us."

"Didn't he try to ask you out a couple years ago?" I asked.

"He wasn't serious," Ember insisted. "Besides, he was a huge player back then, going after all the preppy types. We really are just friends now. Besides, I thought we were talking about Layla and Dash."

I gulped down the huge swallow I'd taken, nearly choking myself. "There's nothing to talk about," I replied.

"Sure, you keep telling yourself that," Ember said.

* * *

GIRL'S NIGHT always left me feeling replenished, if not more than a little tipsy and lacking some of my usual inhibitions. Which is why, as I stumbled out of the elevator, I screeched to a halt short of my door when I came face-to-face with Dash.

God, he looked good enough to eat.

He hadn't noticed me getting off the elevator as his eyes were glued to his phone. I didn't mind. It gave me time to ogle him before we began our usual battle of wills. Pausing at the entrance to the hall, I did just that.

It wasn't fair that someone so frustrating could be so damn handsome.

It gave me a heavy feeling in my stomach that increased with each step. I wanted him. I wanted him more than I could admit to myself and certainly more than I'd be willing to admit to him. I'd been so certain I was going to tell him to back off, to go back to the way things were and then I saw him, and rational thought evaporated.

He looked up as I came to a stop in front of him, the dark slash of his hair across his brow. "Hey," he said, but there was a heaviness in his expression that didn't match his carefree smile.

I tried to concentrate through the flush of alcohol. "Hey, were you waiting for me?" I wasn't sure if I wanted him to be or not.

"Yeah, I was. Can we talk?"

"If we do it at your place?"

His eyes crinkled in a real smile. "Mine? Why?"

I lifted a shoulder. "Because you've been in mine. Don't

pretend you haven't snooped. If we're going to talk, I figure it would only be fair if you let me snoop around yours."

He shrugged and a flash of skin winked at his midsection. I tried not to stare. "Yeah, alright. But I'm warning you, it's probably a mess compared to yours."

"I don't care."

In fact, I didn't think I cared about anything less. He jerked his chin back to the elevator and we rode the short trip to his floor in charged silence. With each passing second, I knew the likelihood I'd come out of this—whatever it was—unscathed, diminished more and more. Maybe taking a chance on Dash wasn't worth the risk, but what was life without a little risk? I'd been playing it safe for so long, maybe it was time for me to crash and burn.

"You and the girls have fun?" he asked to fill the void.

I thought back to our conversation, or inquisition, rather. "Normally, it is, but we all have a lot going on at the moment. It's nice to have them to talk to, though."

He nodded, then dug a hand in his pocket for his keys, which jingled merrily as he fit them in the lock. My heart pounded in my ears and I swore the combination of alcohol and anticipation had the temperature around me rising like maintenance had decided to bump up the heat to sauna level. To distract myself from the nerves, I peered over Dash's shoulder and into the depths of his apartment.

Would it be like the guys' dorms I'd ventured into to work on projects? Cluttered with yesterday's takeout containers and last week's gym shorts. Or would it be barren, somehow lacking personality and empty. The quintessential bachelor's pad. I've been in his apartment before, dozens of time when it was Charlie's, but I didn't think he'd be into the cozy, chick vibe she tended to go for.

"Want something to drink?" he asked as he ushered me inside. "Beer or I can make you a drink, whatever you want."

"Beer is fine, whatever you have." More alcohol didn't sound like a good idea, but I needed something, anything, to wet my suddenly desert-dry tongue.

He moved to the kitchen, which gave me time to study his space. The last time I'd seen it, we'd been packing for Charlie to move out. It had been a husk of a place with boxes and the gaping mouths of bare cabinets. In the time since he moved in, he certainly put his mark on it.

Our complex featured a lot of exposed brick and really great hardwood floors, but that's where the similarities between our two places ended. The accent wall in the living room had been painted a slate gray to compliment the darker tones of the sectional. A flannel blanket was draped over the foot of the chaise end with a closed MacBook on top. Framed, matted artwork hung behind it. I slipped off my shoes and stepped onto the deep, plush rug in a dark burgundy and wondered if I'd see his bedroom tonight. So far, his apartment was nothing like I'd expected, if I were being honest. The kid who used to tease me in class had grown up. What else was there about Dash that had changed that I didn't know about?

He brought me a beer and I drank thirstily, the cool liquid soothing my dry throat. "Thank you. Nice place you have here."

I gestured with my beer bottle to the console table he used for his TV. It was the same dark burgundy as his rug. He was more color-coordinated than I was. "Want to put something on?"

Lifting a shoulder, he said, "I don't have to, but we can if you want."

"I just need something for background noise."

At that, his eyes crinkled. "Feeling nervous, Lay?"

I rolled my eyes. "What did you want to talk about?" I asked instead of answering.

Dash settled on some sort of competitive cooking show, but kept the volume low for background noise. He pulled me to the sectional and ran his free hand through his hair. "I don't know exactly how to say this, so I'm just going to come right out with it."

Oh, God he was going to break it off. Not that there was anything to break off, but I guess if I needed a sign to tell me how I felt, then I got it. I liked Dash. The thought of him breaking it off made my throat sting. I glanced at the door and considered making a run for it, but then he was speaking again, and I was frozen to the spot, the beer turning to acid on my tongue.

"We're playing a dangerous game here, Lay. As your T.A., it's wrong of me to think the things I do, to want the things I want. I could lose my job. You could fail the class. I know how hard you've worked, and it was selfish of me to put that in jeopardy. The last thing I want to do is hurt you, no matter what you may think of me." He said the last statement looking into my eyes. If this was some sort of trick, it was working.

"What are you saying?" I asked once I could unstick my tongue.

"I'm saying..." He trailed off to take a bolstering swallow from his beer, his gaze darting off. He cleared his throat and looked back at me. "I'm saying, we can either keep going as we are and risk it, or we need to end it. I can handle the moral and ethical ramifications. I don't plan on showing you any favor, if anything I'm tougher on you than most, but I don't want to put you in that position. I can handle them, but I don't want you to if you can't."

Whatever I was expecting him to say, it wasn't that. "I could drop the class."

Dash lifted a hand, trailed the back of his hand over my cheek, then traced his thumb over my bottom lip. "I want you, Layla. But I won't let you risk your education for me. You've worked too hard."

"You're talking about risking your job for me," I pointed out. "There's no use arguing. No matter which way you slice it, furthering our relationship while you're my teacher is wrong."

He nodded, though his expression fell. "You're right. Of course, you're right."

I took his beer in my hand and set it along with mine on the side table. In the process, I scooted closer, put my other hand on his thigh. "Maybe sometimes it's good to be wrong," I said, though it was barely a whisper.

His protests, if there were any, were drowned out by my lips. He let me kiss him for one moment, two, then his hands were at my biceps, pushing me away. "Layla, sweetheart, we can't."

To hell with caution, with overthinking. For once, I was going to leap, to fly. "I want to. Just once. If it's too much, we can call it off. But I want to know, at least one time."

His eyes widened with comprehension and he choked out, "Are you sure?" Then he shook his head, lifted a hand. "Never mind, don't answer that. I don't want you to change your mind. That was the only noble moment you'll probably get from me."

I smiled impishly. "Good, then I know you've gone back to normal."

"Quiet," he ordered and coaxed me forward with a hand on my waist. "C'mere." He his lips were cool from the ice-cold beer, but his touch was warm, and his heart thudded underneath my palm where it lay on his chest.

When I pulled back it was to try and catch my breath. My cheeks ached from smiling. If this was what it meant to feel bad, then it didn't feel bad at all. It felt sinful, wicked.

Addictive.

"Show me your room," I said with a voice that sounded nothing like my own.

CHAPTER FOURTEEN

DASH

ONE OF US WAS A VIRGIN, and it wasn't me. As I led her down the hallway to my room, I sure as hell felt as nervous as one.

My bed was unmade from that morning. I had clothes strewn all over the floor. If I'd known she'd see it, I would have straightened up my room before inviting her over. I'd planned on warning her, explaining why the two of us were a bad idea, not inviting her to bed.

She deserved so much better than me.

Layla turned and sat on the edge of my bed, not seeming to notice the surrounding mess at all, despite my worries. She only had eyes for me.

Overcome, I stepped forward between her legs and brought her lips up to mine. She was sweet, so sweet. Once I tasted my fill, I said, "You are so beautiful." The words were more serious than I intended. I meant to seduce her, to charm her, but she charmed me.

"I think I remember you saying I looked like a boy in his sister's dress once," she said with a laugh that crinkled the corners of her eyes. Unable to resist, I kissed her there, too. On my gravestone it would say, *Here lies Dashiel Hampton. He could not resist her.*

"That's only because you'd beaten me at the chess tournament and I was bitter. I got distracted that day because that dress was see-through. I couldn't stop looking at you."

She slapped at my chest. "It was not!"

I nipped at her lips again and inched her backward. "Okay, maybe it wasn't, and I was staring so hard because I hoped it would be."

She stretched out on my bed, as languid and relaxed as a feline, and I crawled in next to her. "If you hadn't been such a dick all this time, maybe this would have happened before."

"No, I'm glad it didn't. I wouldn't have appreciated you then."

"And you appreciate me now?" she asked, her blue eyes twinkling up at me.

Tucking her hair behind her ear, I said, "Why don't I show you?"

Her pupils dilated, and she licked her lips. "Why don't you?"

I meant to go slow, draw it out and make it good for her the way she deserved, but the wildcat underneath me had zero patience. The girl who'd been so cautious in every other aspect of her life was a woman with no patience in bed. Her hips buck underneath me and her kiss has an edge of hunger that entices me to satiate.

Taking her hands, I grinned. "Don't rush me, Ms. Tate."

She threw her head back. "I'm not rushing you," she said. Then, she wrapped her arms around me, tightening her legs around my hips.

I was lost to her. A better man would have told her this wasn't the perfect moment. Then again, a better man wouldn't have pursued her in the first place, wouldn't have driven her to madness, wouldn't have bullied and teased her. A better man would deserve her, but there was no way in hell I'd give anyone else the chance to try.

Maybe that's why I liked to toy with her so much. She was always so damn perfect, so put-together and sure of herself. That's one thing I wasn't. I might act like I had my shit together, like I knew what I was doing, but I had no fucking clue. Then I'd see her, and it was like I was being pulled in her direction. I had to make her look at me, notice me. I'd been willing to do whatever it took to get her attention. Now that I had it, I was afraid the wrong move would make her change her mind.

I wouldn't give her the chance.

She'd had plenty to walk away, to come to her senses.

Now, she was mine.

I let her pull me down to her, let her wrap me as tight as she wanted. It was almost as though she was afraid I *would* leave, but she didn't need to worry. I wasn't going anywhere.

Her ferocity took me by surprise. She was in the submissive

position, but *she* was the one kissing *me*. I took a moment to catch up, but then I was with her, battling her like we'd been doing for years. I welcomed her assault, letting her taste and her hands explore. The places where she touched tingled in her wake, although they were perfectly innocuous. Places like the back of my neck where my hair brushed the collar of my shirt. The inside curve of my elbow. The skin exposed by the neck of my button-up shirt.

Our bodies tangled together, and I wasn't sure I wanted to spend another moment any other way. I lifted one of her legs around my hip, the other entwined around my calf. We fought against each other to get closer. The seam of her jeans caught against my belt buckle and I heard her breath catch. It inspired the same effect as if she'd touched me.

Beneath me, she shuddered and gasped, her hips rising to meet me as though from instinct. As I teased her with nips and strokes, she grew restless. I tried to keep my head clear, tried to take my time, but she would dip her fingers beneath my shirt or claw at my belt buckle and lost myself, my head swimming with thoughts of sex, of her naked. God, I wanted her naked beneath me.

I didn't know if I said the words out loud. I may have, considering feeling her below me was driving me so out of my mind I couldn't think straight. Either way, she shrugged out of her shirt, then undid the clasp of her bra.

Whatever marginal leash I had on my control snapped at the sight of her, bare before me. Her hands tangled in my hair as I dove forward. If I thought I'd lost control before, it was nothing compared to the wildness that came over me as I tasted her skin.

Layla's sighs turned to moans as I teased her and all too soon the little seduction scene I had planned devolved. I panted against her skin and her head twisted back and forth against the pillow. Her hands tugged at my shirt, but I wasn't in a hurry to stop what I was doing.

"Please," she whispered. And that was all it took for me to realize there was an ambrosia more alluring than her sounds of pleasure. Hearing her beg became my new favorite pastime.

I let her peel off my shirt and toss it aside, but only because her pleading took on a frantic edge. Her hands painted designs on my back, carving her desires with her fingernails. I hissed out a breath against her skin as I tried to wrangle back control.

With impossible care, I dragged her jeans down from her hips revealing inch by inch of passion-pink flesh. I shed my own, but left on my briefs because feeling her completely bare beneath me was a sure-fire way for this to end before it even began..

"I'm sorry," she said abruptly, as I was filling my hands with her soft, feminine curves.

"What's that?" I asked. Her scent was driving me to distraction.

"I'm sorry—you know, for not being as... experienced." She didn't meet my eyes when I laid down beside her. The vulnerability that emanated from her urged a primal instinct inside of me to stroke her, to pet her until she relaxed underneath my hands.

"You don't need to apologize, sweetheart. I'm glad you chose me. Honored, even, if that doesn't sound too much like a douchebag." I paused for a second, then gave a mental shrug. She was being as vulnerable as a woman could ever be, maybe more, considering our past. Maybe I owed her the same. "A part of me was glad to hear that you'd never been with anyone. I like the thought of you being all mine."

She smiled. "All yours, huh?"

"Too much?" I asked.

She could have said yes, could have called me any number of names for presuming to have any claim to her, but she didn't. "Is that what you want?"

"For you to be mine?" Even the words caused me to choke up.

Her bravery faltered, as did her gaze. "Yeah," she said looking down at my chest where my heart was racing wildly.

"Part of me wants that more than anything."

She glanced back up. "And the other?"

"The other part is scared of hurting you."

"You won't hurt me, Dash. You've always been honest, sometimes brutally so. Maybe that's why I'm not scared." She looked up at me from underneath long lashes. "Are you going to make me wait any longer?"

My whole body shuddered. I wrestled myself back under control and arranged her on the bed beneath me. She trembled, but her muscles turned to liquid beneath my hands when I slid down between her legs and tasted her. I groaned against her skin, somehow knowing her flavor would haunt me. Her legs tightened around my head as I carefully worked at her clit. Quick flutters, long licks.

She was like a drug I couldn't seem to stop once I started.

When she broke, my fingers dug into her hips to keep her from bucking me off. I kissed the inside of her thighs, her stomach. I wanted to kiss her everywhere I could reach.

"Please," she whispered.

"I like to hear you beg," I said as I moved up her body.

Her eyes were glassy with desire. I brushed back her hair from her face and waited, hovering over her, until they focused on me. She smiled faintly, her arms twining around my neck.

Layla slipped her fingers under the band of my briefs and my brain went blank. Would I ever get used to having her hands on me? She kept going until her fingers were tight around my cock.

"Probably the only time you'll ever hear it," she said.

"I don't think I'd mind that so much." It took me a minute to get the full sentence out. She'd worked my briefs down my hips and I toed them off. I'd never be able to see her again without thinking about having her naked and willing.

Naked and willing and *mine*.

I kissed her slowly, more for my benefit than hers. The second she got her hands on me, it took everything I had not to go off. Not because it had been a while, but because it was *her*. She'd ruined me.

Maybe I was about to ruin her. Maybe that made me as bad as she'd always thought.

Maybe I didn't care.

She braced her hands on my shoulders, her nails biting into my flesh. I smoothed away the wrinkle in her brow with my lips and said, "Let me get a condom." More to remind myself than inform her.

"I want to," she said, and grabbed the condom from my hands after I retrieved it from the nightstand. I didn't have the chance to stop her and had to grit my teeth as she ripped the wrapper with her teeth and then slowly worked it over my cock. Sweat beaded at my hairline and prickled along the backs of my knees.

She was going to be the death of me.

"I'll take it slow," I said when I caught my breath.

"I trust you," she said, and I didn't realize I'd been waiting to hear those words until relief coursed through me.

Poised above her, I fitted myself to her entrance and observed her expression to make sure I wouldn't hurt her more than I had to. Her eyes were closed, but she nodded and said, "It's okay. I want you to," when I paused with the tip of my cock barely inside her.

Who'd have thought I'd need the encouragement?

"Open your eyes," I said, without thinking, the words ripped from the depth of my chest. I was losing control—or she was taking it. "I want to see you."

I saw in her eyes the girl I'd admired, hated, feared, and worshipped. Felt her open and give all she was. She was sweet, tender, and mine.

I groaned as I slipped inside the slightest inch, clenched by the swollen fist of her flesh so tightly I thought I'd be trapped there. I didn't seem to mind the thought.

"Yes." She sighed. "You feel... *God*, you make me feel so good."

"Fuck," I said on an exhalation, pulling back to clear my thoughts and realizing it was a mistake. The friction was almost too much to handle, too sweet to resist.

She shifted, lifted her hips, searching for more. "Please." Hearing her beg only pushed my closer to the edge. "More."

I did as she asked, but only because staying still was near torture. Breath tore from my chest as I sank deeper inside. Fuck, I could feel the entire head of my cock swallowed by her wetness, could feel the pleasure of it shoot through my balls and up my spine. Sweat spread over my back and chest at the effort to maintain a tenuous grip on my control.

Her face pinched as I worked deeper and deeper inside of her with each thrust. She bit her lip and arched her neck. "Okay?" I asked.

She was still for a moment before she let out a breath, nodded. "I'm okay. It's just—a lot. Different."

"Tell me what you want. I want to make it good for you."

She shuddered underneath me, gripped her legs tight, and then rocked her hips up. "I want more."

I froze, her movements having caught me off guard. "More?" I choked out. More might kill me.

"You're not hurting me. I want it. Keep going."

"I said don't rush me."

The gentle in and out was taking me slightly deeper with

each thrust, but she was having a little trouble taking me all the way. To be honest, I knew the long, slow drag inside the tight grasp of her pussy would be more than I could handle, and I wanted to make it good for her.

"I'm not, I just... *please*."

"We're going to go nice and easy, sweetheart. I can feel how much you want it, how deep you're taking me. Oh, fuck, you feel good."

Her head thrashed against the pillow. "Dash, please."

"No, you're going to listen to me for once."

"I am, I promise I am." She whimpered and lifted her hips to meet mine, sending stars shooting across my vision as I slipped deeper inside her.

"Fuck, baby, you can't do that. I'm already a goner here."

I licked my finger tasting sweat and musk and reached between us to stroke the stiff bundle of her clit. Her reaction was instantaneous. She clenched even tighter around me, both inside and out, then loosened, her legs lifting, opening. I cursed and buried my face in her hair.

My strokes lengthened until I was plunging nearly all the way inside her. She lifted her hips to meet me, searching for the friction provided by my finger against her clit. With a soft, beseeching cry, she gripped my hips with her hands and pulled me tight to her. One slick thrust, then I was all the way inside, her thighs cradling my hips.

Her moan broke, then held, her head thrown back, mouth wide. I kissed her throat, nipped with my teeth breathing heavily against the throbbing pulse beating against my lips. I trembled above her to keep still. She was rapture and damnation all at once.

"Okay?" I asked again.

"No," she answered. "Dash, I don't—" She lifted her hips to finish her thought, searching for fulfillment just out of reach.

"I've got you," I said. I increased pressure with my finger against her clit, then moved slowly, rhythmically. Seducing her to the edge as much as I was myself with quick, hard thrusts, and slow withdrawals. It was a torment and a tease.

I wanted to come more than anything, but I wanted to see her first. Wanted to watch the wave of pleasure crash over her, watch her lose it in my arms. My arms shook with the effort to hold my orgasm back, but I kept the pace, studied her reaction until I found a spot that made her writhe beneath me.

She came, wrapped around me like she never wanted to let me go. Like being anchored to me is what allowed to her to fly. I watched as her mouth turned into an "O" of surprise and a flush spread over her chest. Her nipples beaded up, and I tasted them, flinging her higher, sending her soaring.

Then, she said my name on a sigh and sent me tumbling after her.

CHAPTER FIFTEEN

LAYLA

I COULDN'T STOP SMILING It wouldn't take Charlie or Ember long to figure out what had happened, but I didn't care.

Dash was still asleep in front of me and I was wrapped around him like a starfish. It was the weekend, so we didn't have any classes. I was glad to have a few more moments with him where reality didn't intrude. The thought had me hugging him a little tighter until he chuckled and turned around to face me.

"Trying to smother me already?" he asked.

I pressed my face into the warmth of his chest, let the dusting of hair tickle my nose along with the scent of him, sleepy and warm. "Not today," I answered.

"Sex makes you compliant. Good to know," he said, and I could hear the smile in his voice.

"You're lucky I'm feeling so relaxed or you'd have a fist in your stomach right about now," I replied.

"Did you have anything planned for today?" he asked. His thumb lazily trailed up my wrist, causing me to shiver.

"Nothing important."

"Good, then you're mine for the day." I felt a little thrill at the words "you're mine" but decided not to read too much into them.

"What do you want to do?" I asked.

His hand skimmed playfully down my back to cup my ass. "First, I want to get you in the shower, then it's a surprise."

The wicked glint in his eye was intriguing. No one had ever planned a surprise for me aside from Charlie and Ember. Certainly not family. And definitely not any guy. "What kind of a surprise?"

He flicked my nose then rolled out of bed. "Now, Ms. Tate, it wouldn't be a surprise if I told you, would it?"

I took a moment to watch him walk naked to turn on the shower. There was a reason all the girls had gone for Dash in high school and part of it most definitely had to do with his body. Well-muscled thighs, tight, round butt. Broad shoulders coupled with strong arms. The tingle between my legs coupled with a touch of rawness made me groan. I pressed my thighs together, but the sensation didn't abate. In fact, it made it worse. It was the definition of an ache, but a good one. I'd wanted him before, but it was nothing compared to how much I wanted him now.

Flinging the covers off of me, I padded into the bathroom where Dash was already under the spray. Before joining him in the shower, I quickly brushed my teeth and rinsed with mouthwash. I'd already let him see me at my most vulnerable, but I wasn't ready to subject him to my morning breath.

That finished, I opened the curtain and stepped into the shower. Dash made room for me, cocooning my body underneath the torrent of blessedly warm water. He pressed my body against him and kneaded out the soreness in my arms, back and even down to my thighs. My sharp inhalation didn't deter him from working out the lingering soreness and when he finished, my body may as well have been feather-light.

"How are you feeling?" he asked.

"Keep doing that and I'll be perfect."

With care, he squirted a handful of gel into his hands, then spread it over my skin. I made a sound of surprise and squealed, "Boy soap!" but that didn't stop him from covering me with pine scented suds.

He paid particular attention to my nipples, tweaking them between his thumb and forefinger, which stifled all of my protests. When I ran my hands over his body, he turned me around and pressed my back to his chest, so I couldn't reach him. I groaned in frustration, but I quickly forgot my dismay as his hands wandered down to pay special attention between my legs.

I braced myself against him as he detached his showerhead from the post, surprised when I realized it came in two pieces. With a few adjustments, the stationary head was soon jetting out in sporadic pulses, which made my skin warm, then tingle with awareness. With the extendable showerhead, he set the spray to a single, gentle stream.

He directed the stream of water between my legs where he used it, along with his hands, to soothe any tenderness. The strength of his body kept me from falling into a puddle at his feet. When he deemed me sufficiently clean, he said, "How do you feel now?" in a dark, low voice that made me shiver.

"I want you," I said and felt as though my words could have dissolved along with the steam.

Dash kissed my throat. "Not yet, you're still too sore, but I will give you something. Does it ache, sweetheart?"

I nodded, unable to form words.

"I'll take care of it."

I don't know how it happened, how he became the one to soothe when he'd always caused so much torment.

He directed the stream of gently pulsing water at my clit and my knees gave way. He braced my body against his chest, otherwise I would have melted to the floor. One hand cupped the tender weight of my breast and the pad of his thumb rasped against the sensitive nipple. My head, too heavy for me to hold upright, relaxed against his shoulder and my eyes fluttered closed. Breathing the steamy air was nearly impossible, but who needed to breathe, anyway?

The spray of water, like his hard body behind me, was impossible to escape. But I liked that I had nowhere to go, liked that when I strained against him, he held me in place. Possibly, I shouldn't like being restrained. I'm sure there's some feminist part of me that should be outraged at his presumption, but I liked it too much to give a damn.

I was already so sensitized from the night before it didn't

take me long to reach a fever pitch. My moans echoed off the tile walls and his whispered encouragements tickled my ear. His free hand snaked between us, pausing to cup my ass, then slid between my spread thighs in a rear assault. His fingers probed my entrance and I winced a little at the sensation. It didn't hurt much. I let him trace my opening, loving it with his touch.

"Does it hurt?"

I shook my head against his shoulder. "No, I like it."

He filled me with one finger, enough so I could feel him and not be overwhelmed by the sensation. It stung a little, but I relished the burn. It was the perfect complement to the gentle waves of pleasure from his attention to my clit. But it wasn't either that pushed me over the edge. It was his taunting in my ear. His words. Him.

Maybe it had always been him.

"Dash," I whispered uncertainly as I crested.

His arms tightened around me, like he knew I needed his reassurance. "I'm right here. I've got you. Fuck, I wish I could see your face. I want to fill you up all over again."

My vision dotted with black and my whole body shook. Carefully, he removed his finger, replaced the showerhead, and turned me in his arms to cradle me against his chest until the trembling ceased and my breathing returned to normal.

I reached for him, but he stopped my hand before I could wrap it around his cock. Looking up at him quizzically, I asked, "What's wrong?"

Dash shook his head. "Nothing, but if you touch me, I'm gonna want more and we should wait a while. Don't worry,

NICOLE BLANCHARD

feeling you come all over my hand was enough for me." His blunt talk made me blush, but it also made me want him more. I must have shown it in my expression because he laughed. "Let's get some clothes on and get somewhere public before my dick overrules my common sense."

* * *

"WHERE ARE WE GOING?" I asked as we got in the elevator.

After he'd helped me wobble from the shower, then dried me carefully with a fluffy towel, I'd waited for him to dress. Okay, maybe I ogled him as he did. It really wasn't fair. He made jeans and a long-sleeved shirt look attractive and he didn't even have to try!

Once he dressed, he followed me back to my place and I'd tried to convince him to give me a hint about where we were going, but he wouldn't budge. I nixed his suggestion of a little black dress that barely skimmed my thighs and chose jeans and a light sweater that complimented my eyes. The jeans may or may not have been skin tight. From the look in his eye they drove him a little crazy, which I felt was appropriate.

Later, I'd think about the consequences from my actions. Later.

Today, I would forget the rules and enjoy.

"For a ride," Dash said mysteriously.

I rolled my eyes. "To where?"

"You let me worry about that," he answered.

136

He took my hand as we left the elevator and journeyed through the shadowed parking garage to where his Jeep was parked. He unlocked it, opened the door for me, then helped me up into the lifted seat. His hands lingered on my hips, then he gave me a teasing grin and climbed into the driver's seat.

Whatever, if he wants to chauffer me around town, then fine by me. My mother was due for a drop-by soon, especially since I hadn't given her any indication that I'd done as she'd asked and applied to Kragen's. I had no urge to be home when she did, which I'd certainly hear about later, but I didn't care. My whole life had been about catering to someone else's whims instead of my own. Today, I would do what I wanted.

It made me want to laugh that what I wanted most of all was to spend it with Dash.

I shook my head at the absurdity as he reversed out of the parking space. How times had changed.

Casually, liked he'd been doing it for years, Dash's hand found its way to my thigh as he navigated into traffic. It made my heart skip a beat, then jump into my throat. We'd done far, far more than the simple contact of his hand resting on my skin, but the affection was unexpected.

"Something wrong?" he asked, glancing over at me.

All at once I realized I'd never had affection like this. Not from my mother. Not from Delia. I could barely even remember my father. I didn't even know it was something I'd been missing until Dash did it without a thought.

An ache burned at the back of my throat, but I forced

myself to speak normally. The radio was up, so I hoped he couldn't hear the quaver in my voice. "No, everything's great."

He zoomed up and down the hilly terrain and wound his way through traffic, all while touching me. A hand knotted with mine. My fingers pressed to his lips. His grazing my cheek during stop lights. If he was a drug, I was high on him. By the time we pulled to a stop, hunger had extinguished my curiosity. He'd given me a taste and I wanted more.

His eyes were as hot as the fire burning inside me. "Don't you want to know where we are?"

I jumped the distraction. Breathing heavily, I turned away from the magnetic pull of his gaze and grappled to regain my balance. I recognized the parking lot and the red brick and white columned building. "The library?" I said, my tone laced with bewilderment.

Of all the places I would have guessed he'd take me, the public library hadn't been one. He unbuckled, then rounded the front of the Jeep to open my door. Every time he did something nice for me it was like a shock of electricity that coursed through my body. Not only because he'd always done the opposite, but because I couldn't remember someone other than my friends being so thoughtful.

"Do you have something against libraries?" he asked, taking my hand and helping me down.

"No, of course not." It was the middle of the day and the parking lot was nearly empty. It crossed my mind that there was a slim possibility we'd run into someone from school, but I didn't want to think about that yet. "What are we doing here?"

"You ask so many questions," was his only answer.

Normally, I valued being in charge. I liked knowing what would happen, when, and how, but I had to admit it gave me a little thrill not knowing what he had planned. I followed as he bounded up the steps and held the door open for me. He made a beeline for the help-desk and gave the woman behind it a dazzling smile. I hid my own as he retrieved a handful of scrap paper from a basket on the counter and two stubby pencils. Apparently even married librarians weren't immune to Dash's charm.

He herded me across the room toward the maze of shelves and handed me half the scrap paper and a pencil.

"Okay?" I said with a raised brow. "Don't tell me you brought me here for homework."

"Don't tempt me. No. When I was younger, my mom liked to bring me here. We'd write notes and put them in our favorite books for the next person to read. After they moved to Washington for my dad's campaign, I'd come here whenever I missed them, and I'd look through all her favorite books to see if I could find any notes she'd written. Your mission, should you choose to accept it, is to write notes and leave them in your favorites. Last one finish buys lunch."

"You're crazy," I said with a laugh, then added, "But you're on."

Without waiting for his response, I booked it to the end of the aisle, already hunting for the titles of my favorite books. I'd never known he used to do this with his mother. It humanized him turned him from the guy who'd been my enemy to something more. What else did I have to learn about him?

I searched through the rows of books, lost for a while in the memories that arose with each one. Anne of Green Gable, Charlotte's Web, The Secret Garden. The notes were a combination of life advice and things I'd wish someone had told my younger self, specifically, things I'd wished my own mother had said instead of the constant litany of 'you're not good enough.'

When I finished, I glanced up and didn't see Dash anywhere around. Curious and feeling a little competitive, I snug around the shelves searching for him. I found him in the chapter book section a couple rows away. He hunched over a battered copy of The Hobbit, which made me smile. I could picture him reading it, engrossed. He carefully tucked the slip of paper into the pages and replaced the book on the shelves.

He glanced up and I threw myself behind the shelves, not wanting him to catch me staring at him. I peered above a row of books and watched him amble down the end of the row and out of sight. A few more seconds passed without him returning. Ears straining, I crept down the row to the place where I saw him put the book back and scanned the titles until I came to The Hobbit.

The cracked spine whispered as I opened it. The pages rustled open to Dash's handwriting.

There is some good in this world, and it's worth fighting for.

- J.R.R. Tolkein

I did the same thing when I found him on the next aisle. This time, it was a copy of Alice in Wonderland. It's note read:

It's no use going back to yesterday, because I was a different person then.
- Lewis Carroll

These words had touched Dash, the guy who'd mercilessly teased me, who'd been the bane of my existence growing up. I couldn't help but feel like they were a message. Maybe I'd been the person who needed to read them.

Competition forgotten, I ambled up and down the aisles lost in thought until Dash found me wandering around the picture book section. "There you are!" he spotted the papers in my hand. "Looks like you owe me lunch!"

I gave him a small smile, but I couldn't seem to look him in the eye. "Guess so. Where do you want to go?"

He lifted a shoulder. "Wherever you want. I'm not picky if you're treating."

I made to move passed him, but he stopped me. "What?"

"Did it hurt?"

Laughing, I shook my head and stepped away. "Dash, no."

He blocked my exit. "C'mon, sweetheart. Be a good sport."

I turned away so he couldn't see my smile. He didn't need any encouragement. "I don't think so."

Dash nipped at the underside of my jaw, causing my breath to catch. "Pretty please?" His voice was low, intimate. Like it had been last night when he spoke those sweet, sexy words in my ear.

"Fine. Let me guess. When I fell from heaven? I hate to break it to you, Dash, but I'm no angel."

He presses a kiss to my lips. If it had a taste, it would have been sugar-sweet. "No, did it hurt when you fell for me?"

The denial is immediate and overwhelming, a wave that swelled in my chest and washed away all my thoughts. "Stop it," I said, my voice almost a whisper and smile turning to a frown.

It was too much. I couldn't handle the feelings that had taken root inside of me the night before. Not when he'd charmed his way through my defenses, then completely disarmed me today.

If this was war...he was winning.

"Stop what?"

I squirmed away, but he pulled me right back. Despite everything inside of me telling me to fight, to run, to hit back like I'd always done when it came to him, something stopped me. A part of me wanted to hear what he had to say next. After seeing all the sides of him I'd never known existed, maybe there was a new side of me, too. One that wanted Dash more than it wanted self-preservation. I swallowed hard.

"Teasing me."

"I'm not teasing you." He lowered his voice even more. "You'd know it if I was."

Instead of answering, I reached for him. Took the kiss I'd been craving since we left his apartment. It was a little desperate, yearning. It took the line between love and hate and blurred it until there was nothing left but shadows.

CHAPTER SIXTEEN

DASH

SHE PUSHED AGAINST MY CHEST, but it was half-hearted, and her fingers twisted the fabric of my shirt. The distance between us shrank the longer the seconds drug on. I regretted bringing her to a public place. At first, it had been because I knew I needed the buffer. It was too easy to fall into her, too easy to get lost in her. If we'd spent any more time alone together, I would have convinced her to get naked again. Convinced her to let me inside her. She'd given me her virginity, but it felt like she'd taken a part of *me* instead.

I stared deep into her eyes, the playful smile on my lips disappearing. "What are you doing to me?" I asked, my tone softening from teasing to questioning.

She flinched, then licked her lips. Her voice was breathy when she answered. I imagined her on her knees, licking her lips like that as she held my dick. She was barely touching me, and I wanted her with a fierceness that superseded common sense. "I'm not doing anything."

She was everything.

"I think about you all the time now," I told her, the words wrenched from my chest like she was my absolution. "Used to be it was because I liked getting a rise out of you. I'll admit, arguing with you is fun. Part of it was knowing you'd be thinking about me for hours afterward."

"I don't think about you for hours," she protested.

I studied the flushed swells of her cheeks and thumbed her red lips. "You think about me so much that's why you're always so fired up when you see me. You think about me so much it pisses you off. You wish you could dismiss me as easily as you claim."

"I can," she says defiantly, tossing back her mane of brown hair. I'd believe her more if her hands weren't roaming over my chest.

"If you could, then what are you doing here with me now?"

Her mouth dropped open and I took advantage of her surprise with a kiss that tempted us both. Lips parted, she moaned against mine, then submitted, her body going lax.

And. I. Fucking. Loved. It.

Watching her fight how much she wanted me and then succumbing to it had to be the hottest fucking thing I've ever experienced. Women have wanted me, chased me, fallen for me, but never, not once, have they fought against it. Tried to run. Not like Layla did. For years I'd been trying to catch her. And, God, how I enjoyed the chase.

"Let's get out of here," she whispered against my lips. Her words tasted of desperation. It would have been easier to say yes. "Let's go back to your place. I want you. Please."

"You only say that because you don't want to have to think about what's going on between us. You want to run away from what's happening here just like you're always running from me. Sex is easy, it's feelings that are hard."

She pulled away. "Why do we have to complicate it? Life is complicated enough as it is."

"The things in life that are most worth it never come easy. Maybe I think you're worth it." My words steal her protests and while she has time to think, I tugged her toward the exit. "Let's get something to eat. Are you hungry?"

"Really, Dash? You're just going to ignore the whole thing? We have to talk about this." I had to be a bastard because much as I liked her, there was something about hearing the frustration in her voice that brought a satisfied smile to my face. Surprise or disbelief has her pulling away. I glanced back and found her frozen in place.

"I buy you ice cream after lunch. Chocolate fudge, whatever you want. C'mon."

She hesitated for a moment on the edge of indecision, then took my hand. "It'd better be a big one."

* * *

I TAKE her to the Railroad Square Art District, a little bohemian mecca for occultists and obscure art collectors and distributors. Situated in the heart of Tallahassee, it's nestled on a railroad track and shaded by ancient oaks, like much of the rest of the capital city. Funky little businesses occupy candy-colored storefronts. It has everything from a second-hand store to an herbalist to an eco-tourism place.

When I first came to Florida State as an undergrad, I took advantage of the night life. Wasted away thousands of hours trolling the bar scene, the party scene. They didn't call FSU a party school for nothing. Since I've come back, I've spent most of my free time exploring the city for hidden nooks like this one.

"Where are we going?" Layla asked when I came to a stop in a shaded gravel parking area. "Where are we?"

"I told you, I'm taking you to lunch. Then we'll hunt down some ice cream."

"You act like that's going to solve all of our problems."

I shrugged as I helped her out of my Jeep. "You act like ice cream doesn't solve all problems on a regular basis."

She harrumphed, but followed me down the road nonetheless. When I took her hand, she didn't protest. Baby steps.

"There's a little restaurant just over here. It's actually made from the caboose of a train. I think you're really going to like it. They've got good beer and great sandwiches."

As a plus, the area didn't get much business in the middle of the day, so we were unlikely to be spotted by anyone. Campus may be huge, but my father had campaigned enough that it wasn't out of the norm for me to be recognized. Word traveled quickly when you were named one of Tallahassee's Hottest Bachelors. Even more quickly when you were teaching.

"I'm only going with you because I'm hungry," she said, then gasped as we drew closer to the train car.

It was painted a faded red that drew the eye. We approached from the back where a large sign advertised open spots for entertainers. The entrance was on the short side of the car and facing the front was an outdoor seating area under an open-air structure. A small stage was situated under lights that must be stunning at night all lit up.

"This is beautiful," Layla said with a sigh. "It's so cute!"

I held open the door for her. "I thought you might like it. The meatball sub is especially good."

Small two-person tables lined the wall of windows to the left and a bar flanked our right. Layla took a seat at the bar and studied the menu written in colorful chalk on the wall in front of her.

Needing to touch her, I always seemed to have some part of me connected with her, I laid a hand on her shoulder and stood behind her. She rested her cheek, just for a moment, on my hand, then went back to reading.

This.

This was why I kept coming back to her even though experience, common sense, and even the girl herself kept warning me away.

One touch from her struck me deeper than any other. It meant more, made me feel more, than anything else I'd ever known.

The owner finished with another customer and moved down the bar to take our orders. I thumbed Layla's cheek, loving the texture of her skin under my hands, as she ordered a meatball sub and a bottle of water. I got a brat with cucumber salad and a craft beer.

"You can wait here or outside, and I'll bring it right out to you," the owner said.

"Lead the way," I said.

The bit of Indian summer we were experiencing had the temperature at a balmy sixty-nine degrees, so Layla didn't hesitate to step through another door and into the outdoor eating area. Benches peppered the space and she chose the one closest to the door. We were the only ones sitting outside and I was grateful for the privacy. I wasn't quite ready to share her yet. I liked having her all to myself.

"Why are you doing this?" Layla asked after taking a sip from her water. She played with the cap as she spoke, twisting the top on and off.

"Feeding you?" I asked. "I've known you long enough to realize you're better when you're fed."

She rolled her eyes. "After we eat, are we going to discuss what we're going to do about this? And don't play dumb. You know what I'm talking about."

I rested my elbows on the picnic table where we were sitting and nodded. "Sure, we can talk about it. We can talk about it all you like. *After* we eat, and that includes ice cream. I want you in the best possible mood before we have this discussion."

"You just want to tip things in your favor, but I have news for you Dash, lunch and ice cream isn't going to change our situation."

"You never know," I waggled my eyebrows at her. "You haven't had it yet. Let's make a deal: you drop the discussion talk until after we've eaten and when we're done, we can hash things out. I won't dodge and questions and I'll respect whatever decision you come to in the end."

She pressed her lips together, her posture straightening in interest. "Even if I say we can't see each other anymore? Including gettogethers with my friends and those little verbal sparring matches you seem to like so much?"

I nodded in affirmative. "Whatever you decide, I'll respect. Even if it's not what I want."

She hesitated, lifted a shoulder. "I guess I can handle a free lunch and ice cream for that. Why do you care so much?"

"Shouldn't I?" That seemed to stump her. I can't say I didn't enjoy watching her struggle for words.

"If you want to talk, I'll be asking the questions."

I gestured for her to go ahead.

"You'll tell me the truth?" she pressed.

"I've never lied to you, Lay, I don't plan on starting now."

"Why didn't you go into politics like your dad?" It was a question I've gotten several times before—from my friends, family, the press. It's one I normally dodged with a joke and a change of subject.

"Getting right to the good stuff."

She sipped her water. "You promised."

"I guess because I wanted to prove I could make it on my own. If I would have followed in the great Hampton footsteps right away, there would have been no way for me to distinguish myself from the name. I wanted to earn what I get on my own terms."

Layla doesn't comment, but there's no mistaking the smile on her lips. "If you could be anything in the world what would it be?"

I could have answered anything, could have made up something that wouldn't have been so embarrassing, but I didn't. I cleared my throat. "A father." My voice didn't tremble, but I could feel my throat flush.

She choked on her water. "What? Really?"

"Why the tone of surprise?" I asked.

"I guess I never thought about it. Why father?"

I had her whole attention and I couldn't deny having those wide curious eyes wholly devoted to me. I lifted a shoulder. "My grandparents my not be the warmest people in the world, but my parents are wonderful. I had a great childhood growing up. I want what they had. The partnership. The commitment. The family. They only had me, but I think I'd want to have two or three rugrats. What about you?"

"Do I want a family?" She fiddled with the cap of her bottle, readjusted her legs. "I'm not sure, I guess I haven't thought about it much. I've been so focused on school and graduating, there never seemed to be time for anything else."

"I would have thought you'd have it all planned out by now."

She laughed and it lit up her eyes. "Maybe that's the next step after graduation and getting a job. One thing at a time."

"That all you wanted to know?"
"Not even close, Hampton."

CHAPTER SEVENTEEN

LAYLA

A FATHER.

That had been the last answer I'd expected him to give. An entrepreneur, a rockstar, an athlete. Those had been the answers I would have thought he'd give. Something with flash and prestige. A career that would put him in the limelight he so clearly deserved. A father had been nowhere on the list. He may as well have said orangutan.

Once the words came out of his mouth, though, I couldn't stop picturing him toting around babies, joking with smart-mouthed preteens. Kissing a heavily pregnant wife. He'd be a great father. The image shouldn't be so appealing, but it was. I guess that's what people meant when they talked about ovaries exploding.

Family had never equaled happiness to me, not really. It had meant obligation. Guilt. Disappointment. Family had always emphasized the things I lacked.

My sister Delia had never experienced the same, she'd always been the Golden Child, She-Who-Could-Do-No-Wrong. She had my mother's unflinching support and praise and didn't seem to understand why I was always so downtrodden.

"Get over it, Layla. Just do what she says, and she'll leave you alone. If you'd stop arguing with her, she wouldn't be so hard on you."

Delia had never got the verbal abuse I did. She either didn't care or didn't realize it was wrong because it had been the same all of our lives. Maybe she was just grateful she wasn't on the receiving end of one of mom's tongue lashings.

Mom...I'd never felt like family to her. Or she to me. She'd been a dictator, a bully, a drill-sergeant, but never what I thought a mother would be. I'd never known any different until I went to school and was exposed to how other mothers treated their daughters.

Seeing other families together had only underscored the notion that I was the reason we couldn't have a normal relationship. She'd said as much to me often enough that it didn't take long for me to believe her. After all, she was the authority figure, the adult, my parent. Who was I to know any different?

Dash waved a hand in front of my face. "Did I lose you?"

Before I could answer, the owner came out with two plates full of food. The scent of cheese and sauce made my mouth water. He sat our plates in front of us with a flourish. "Can I get ya'll anything else?"

Dash looked to me and I shook my head. "No thank you," he said. "This looks great."

I took a bite of my sub sandwich and groaned. An explosion of fresh bread, thick sauce and sharp cheese coated my tongue. "Oh my god," I moaned.

"Good?"

"So good." I took another bite, then a sip of my water. "So, a dad, huh? I can see that." All too clearly. It made what had happened between us last night all the more...real.

He looked up from his "Oh, you could?"

"I mean I don't think you'd let them die or anything," I quickly corrected.

His laugh made his eyes light up. Seeing it made me want to make him laugh all the time. I liked it almost as much as seeing his expression go stormy with anger or irritation. Maybe there was something to the way he liked to provoke me. Did he feel the same way about me when we were arguing?

"Well, thanks for the vote of confidence." He paused to eat some of the side cucumber salad he'd ordered. "If you could do anything, what would you do?"

I thought about my mom's insistence about the finance job. About the flush of accomplishment and satisfaction I felt during my student teaching hours. There was no comparison. "I'd be a teacher." My mouth moved without conscious thought and I spoke without hesitation coloring my voice.

"Why do you let your mom push you into the business thing, then, if that's not what you really want?"

Stuffing my face with spicy tomato sauce and well-seasoned

meatballs seemed like the best response. He waited patiently, eating his own meal in the meantime. Patience was an quality I'd never considered Dash to possess, but he did in spades. In class, in his personal life, with me.

I ate half my sub before I broke down and answered. "Sometimes it's easier to buckle under and do what she wants so she'll get off my back. She's paying for my degrees, some of my bills. I don't have much of a choice."

"Do you ever stand up to her?" he asked.

Pointing my drink at him, I said, "I thought this was supposed to be my rodeo. I'll be asking the questions."

He made a 'go-ahead' gesture with his brat, but I knew he wouldn't be dropping the subject, simply filing it away for later.

"Why me?"

The question slipped out, again without thought. It was getting too easy for me to drop all my barriers around him. Too easy to let him see and possess parts of me without my permission.

I shook my head at myself, my tongue tangling. "You don't have to answer that. It was a stupid question."

Dash reached across the table, dwarfed my hand with his. "I'll tell you as many times as you need to hear it. I'll keep answering it until you believe me. It's you because it's always been you, even when I didn't want it to be. It's you because as much as you hate me, I know you like me just as much." At my burning look, he laughed and corrected, "Okay, maybe you hate me a little more."

"What are we going to do about this? We both have a lot to lose."

He turned my hand over in his, twined our fingers together. "I don't know what we're going to do. I don't have the answers here anymore than you do. I can tell you what I want."

I finished my sandwich one-handed, almost afraid of asking, but I did because I had to know. I burned for the answer almost as much as I ached for him the night before. "What do you want?" I was nearly breathless with anticipation.

He had no hesitation and his unflinching gaze was on me. I wasn't at all prepared for what he said. "I want to see where this is going to go. I want to get to know you more. I want to see you. And I'm willing to take that as fast or as slow as you want."

"And if I said I thought we should go back to a professional relationship, at least until the semester was over?"

Dash took my plate and empty water bottle, threw it and his own away in the trash. He helped me up from the table and tucked me into his side. "Then, I'd understand, and I'd be patient. You're worth waiting for."

He seemed to realize I needed time to process and we walked hand in hand back to his Jeep after finishing our meal. He closed the door behind me and I buckled myself into the seat as I contemplated his words.

Dashiell Hampton wasn't only the bane of my existence. He was also a talented teacher, a focused student, an aspiring businessman, a loyal son and grandson, and maybe, possibly...the man I was beginning to love.

* * *

HE WAS A WHIRLWIND. There was no other way to describe it. I'd coast along, thinking I had everything planned out, every eventuality carefully plotted and decided, and he'd scoop me up like a tornado and drop me miles away from my previous destination.

Dash wasn't anything like I'd planned. He was so much more.

I wasn't entirely sure how I was going to handle it, until I saw his grandmother, her name was Elizabeth, I remembered, standing at my front door. Much like her grandson had been doing not so long ago.

"Mrs. Hampton," I greeted as I walked across the hall from the elevator. I was all too aware of Dash's taste still lingering on my lips, the ghost of his hands still branding my waist. "Please come in." Whatever it was, it couldn't be good. The look in her eye wasn't congenial, but I motioned in my apartment after unlocking the door. When we were both inside, I asked, "Would you like something to drink? Water, coffee?"

She clutched her purse and shook her head. "No, thank you, I won't be here long."

Anxiety clutched my belly tight. "Well, what can I do for you, Mrs. Hampton?"

"When I met my Edward, I wasn't much different than you. A reasonably attractive woman from an acceptable family attending college for a lucrative degree. I was in law school when we met. Of course, I quit my dream school because I knew what it would take to be a Hampton wife." She pinned me with a hard, unflinching gaze. "Edward's mother Clarissa didn't think I had what it took to be a good wife to her son and if Dashiel's parents weren't so busy on the campaign they'd tell you the same thing. You are not the woman for him, you will never be the woman for him. He needs someone who understands his family, his future, and isn't afraid to go after what she wants, to stand up for herself. You are none of those things."

My back stiffened. Heat painted the base of my neck. "Excuse m-me?" I stammered. "You don't know anything about me." The words barely made their way over my tongue, which had the taste and texture of a baked Nevada highway at noon. The fact that she spoke aloud the fears I didn't even realize I had made my stomach threaten to reject the delicious lunch Dash had treated me to.

She shakes her perfectly coiffed head and smiles knowingly. "I know everything about you, Layla Lucille Tate. I know that you're a Business-Art major, which tells me you can't even make up your mind about what you want with your future, let alone give my grandson the attention and dedication he'll need. Before this gets any more difficult, I'm here to advise you to do the right thing and let him go. Let him go before this affects both of your futures."

I was quite simply, without words. She reminded me so much of my mother, the same self-assured singlemindedness. It didn't occur to her that maybe I was the right person for Dash, even if I wouldn't admit it to myself. It didn't occur to her that it wasn't her place to meddle in our lives. Just like my mother, she thought she thought she could dictate to and micromanage those around her without a protest or complaint.

She started for the door, already certain I would comply with her demands. "I trust we have an understanding?" she said over her shoulder.

Before I could so much as reply, she was out of the door and it swung shut with a smart *click* before I could even unclamp my jaws. I folded limply into a pile on my couch, still staring at the door where Elizabeth Hampton had disappeared, her expensive Chanel perfume still lingering in the air.

I'd barely had time to process the night with Dash, the day, and now this? I couldn't seem to get my head on straight before something crashed in and destroyed what little certainty I'd managed to scrape together. And I couldn't talk to anyone about this.

My friends still didn't know we were together, and I couldn't tell them. Especially not now. Admitting to anyone what had happened would put both of us at risk.

I'd wanted more time to figure things out. To understand how I was feeling.

Time I didn't have.

There wasn't much I thought Dash and I had in common until now. He'd been born into a sterling family name, the proverbial silver spoon in his mouth. He wouldn't have to fight for what he wanted—it was handed to him. A cushy career in politics, a vast family fortune. Status, wealth, prestige. It didn't hurt that genetics had blessed him with a face fit for a prince. He never wanted for anything. Whereas I had to fight for everything. I'd only succeeded so far because I worked for it all. My[NB1] mother liked to put on a mask that we were upwardly mobile, that we had money and she certainly spent it like we did, but when my father abandoned us, he took his bank account with him. We had our name and little else.

But the one thing Dash and I had in common was apparently the women in our lives, pushing, manipulating, orchestrating. Every moment planned, every step carefully mapped out. I had my mother—he had his grandmother. It made me wonder what other parts of his life had been controlled by his family like mine had.

Needing to think, knowing I couldn't let anyone else make the decision for me, I headed for my bathroom and pulled the shower curtain aside. I set the water to steaming hot and let the bath fill as I poured myself a glass of wine and lit candles. I pushed the dilemma to the back of my mind as I poured cherry blossom bubble bath in the running water and stripped. It may have been my imagination, but I could still feel Dash's hands on my bare skin.

By the time I stepped into the water, steam was already curling the ends of my hair and I'd come to a decision.

CHAPTER EIGHTEEN

DASH

IF I THOUGHT it had been worse before, seeing her in class the following week was something akin to hell.

This time, she didn't spend the whole hour ignoring me, pretending I didn't exist. She studied the text as I lectured, took notes—because who was Layla if not the dutiful student?—but in between the notes, her eyes would be on me. They burned with an intensity I'd never seen in her before.

I spent the hour lost in thought, lecturing purely by memory, wondering what was going on behind her stare. Had she decided to walk away? I couldn't necessarily hold it against her if she had. Our timing was shit. Did she blame me? I would. I took advantage her, in more ways than one. Used our history to get her into bed, risking both of our futures.

There wasn't one good reason she should even consider anything I'd said the day before or my carefully reasoned arguements that had gotten her into bed.

Everything was against us. Hell, even I'd done my best to sabotage in the beginning.

By the end of class, if I hadn't written the lecture and given it several times, I wouldn't have known what the hell I talked about. I considered dropping to my knees right there in front of God and everyone and begging. Is that what she wanted? For me to beg? I was more than willing.

Without looking up, I packed my things. I was sure if I did, I'd watch her walk away and I didn't want to tempt myself. Layla hated scenes, being the center of attention. By the time I'd carefully stowed away my laptop, phone, pens, and anything else I could think of to give myself more time, I'd at least gotten my hands to stop shaking.

Christ. What was this girl doing to me?

When I couldn't put it off anymore, I looked up.

And there she was.

Layla.

A knowing smile sat on her lips as though she could read my mind.

When had she become the aggressor in this little scenario?

Probably around the time I got my first taste of her, if I were being honest with myself. Maybe even before that. Maybe it had been the first lashing she'd ever given me with that sweet tongue of hers.

My feet drew me toward her without thought. She stood, shouldered her bag, waited for me.

I stopped when I could scent her. Clean, something simple. Something that invited me closer to find all the places where it lingered on her skin. Do, how I wanted my mouth on her again. I would have given anything to taste her again.

"Mr. Hampton," she greeted soberly.

All I could do was nod.

"Do you have office hours now?" she asked.

I had no idea, but I held out a hand for her to lead the way. If I didn't, I'd cancel whatever class I was supposed to be teaching next.

When I found my voice, I said, "What is it you want to talk about, Ms. Tate?"

I couldn't read her expression. "We can discuss it when we get to your office," was all she'd say.

I followed her out of the lecture hall, through throngs of students, and wondered if I could convince her not to throw us away before we'd even got started. If my friends from high school could see me now, they wouldn't believe the womanizer Dash Hampton was following a woman around like a forlorn puppy dog.

She stood patiently as I unlocked my office door and let her in. It closed behind us with a pronounced thump and I locked it, just in case. With exaggerated care, I placed my bag beside my chair and turned to face her. For the first time, I couldn't read her expression, so I memorized the moment instead.

She was wearing jeans and some sort of sweater combo, one whose neckline dipped just enough to tease at the tops of her breasts and nip in at her waist. Her dark hair tumbled around her shoulders and I wanted to bury my face in her throat where her scent was the strongest.

As I studied her, she sat in the chair across from my desk, crossed her trim legs and knotted her hands in her lap and simply waited, watching me.

"What is it, Lay?" I asked when the silence great to be unbearable.

Was she enjoying this?

The smile that bloomed on her lips said she was. "I thought we should talk."

I relaxed into my chair, feigning a nonchalance I absolutely did not feel. "About what?"

"Us," she said simply and rose from her chair to sit on the edge of my desk, bring her close enough that I could feel her soft heat.

"What about us?"

"After you brought me home, I thought a lot about everything that's happened." Was I imagining it, or did a shadow cross her expression? I tensed as she continued. "I think if we were to continue our relationship right now, it wouldn't end happily. One of us would get hurt or we'd get caught." I opened my mouth to argue, but she held up one slim finger and I shut it. "What we're doing is risky and would have consequences for both of us if we were seen and someone reported it to your superior." She was basically repeating the arguement I'd given her a few days ago.

Although I knew she was right, I couldn't help but protest. "Then we'd be careful."

But she shook her head. "We were already taking a risk yesterday. All it would take is one person. Do you really want to spend the beginning of whatever this is constantly looking over your shoulder, wondering if we're going to get caught?"

What she was saying made sense, hell, I'd told myself the same on several occasions. That didn't mean it didn't suck to hear. Stop being a pussy. "I told you I wouldn't push you into anything, and I won't. Graduating means everything to you and I understand that."

I sounded like one of her academic advisors.

She nodded. "Good. I'm glad we're on the same page."

I wanted to grab her, so I clenched my hands into fists. "Good. Was there anything else you wanted to talk about?"

"No, that about covers it."

How was this so easy for her? I'd never had much of an explosive temper, but the frustration that rose inside of me at her casual tone made me want to rage.

When I spoke, my voice was as rough as gravel. "Was that all?"

Layla straightened, stepped closer. *Christ.* "So we have an agreement?"

I nodded jerkily. "Of course. I'll keep my space. No one has to know what happened. Our relationship from this point on will be purely professional. I should apologize for crossing that line, but I'm not fucking sorry."

"You don't have to apologize. You're not the only one at fault here."

I wished she'd give me some space. There's only a breath of room between us and with her standing in front of me, I'm level with her chest, craning my neck to look up at her. "You're my student. I pushed you and you know it."

"Then we'll just have to wait until I'm no longer in your class. Then you won't have any excuses."

My hands unclenched. "No, I was such a--wait, what?"

She smiled. "Until class is over, we won't see each other outside of the lecture hall. We'll keep our relationship completely platonic--at least until the end of the semester." She lifted a shoulder. "This way we can both cool off and decide if what happened was just hormones and lust or if there's something more there without the risk of putting our futures in jeopardy."

I swallowed and almost choke on my own tongue. "So you aren't breaking things off?"

"Well, sort of. At least until after the semester. No more of those come-fuck-me-looks, no more flirting, no more lingering in the hallway in front of my apartment, and definitely no more kissing."

"No more kissing?" The end of the semester was an eternity away. Weeks at least. Could I last that long?

She shook her head. "None." Her confident tone and expression faltered. "W-what do you think?"

I reached out, took her hand and pulled her onto my lap. Her thighs spread over my legs and I was grateful my desk chair had no arms, allowing her to fit close to me.

"I think if we're going to spend the rest of the semester without any kissing, then I'd better get my fill now."

I covered her mouth with my own and she pressed her

hands against my chest. When she broke apart, I buried my face in her throat.

"What are you doing?" she asked, and it pleased me to find her breathless.

"Paying you back for torturing me a second ago. I thought you were trying to tell me to get lost."

She made an impatient sound as my lips captured her ear lobe. "I am, sort of. We shouldn't be doing t-this here. That was the whole point."

"I locked the door. No one is getting in and my next class doesn't start for an hour. If I can't have you until next year, then I need one last kiss to hold me over." My mouth traversed a languid path back to hers. "We'd better make it a good one."

She melted over me in the way I liked so much and her lips softened, opened, over mine. At the submission, my tongue delved into her sweetness, urging hers to battle. I rubbed mine against hers until her hands lifted to grip either side of my face. She took over the kiss, tinder to flame.

"That's enough," I said and pulled away. Too much more and we'd have more reason for the locked door. "You should go now."

But her blue eyes had gone bright with hunger and she shifted restlessly on my lap.

"Maybe you were right, about one more time," she said thoughtfully. Her gaze followed her hand as she toyed with the collar of my shirt, her fingers fluttering over the exposed skin.

"I said one more kiss."

"Are you asking me to stop?" Before I had a second to reply

she was lifting her shirt over her head. All of her carefully reasoned arguements evaported as creamy flesh filled my vision. The thin bralette she wore underneath did little to hide the flushed rose of her nipples. My mouth watered and shifted to get her off my lap, but she beared down on my, grinding down against the growing hardness.

"Layla," I said between gritted teeth. "You should go." My hands made me a liar as they gripped her hips to work her over my erection. The layers of fabric did nothing to disguise the paradise between her legs. Her heat burned through both our jeans and made my thoughts turn muddled.

"I will," she said and got to her feet. Dual edges of relief and despair had me reaching for her, then rubbing my eyes and wishing for a cold beer.

When I dropped my hands, my spine stiffened. "Layla, what the hell are you doing?"

She didn't answer, and didn't need to. The sound of her jeans dropping to the floor was answer enough. I protested and then she tucked her thumbs in the waistband of her panties and pushed them over her hips. The sight made it damn near impossible to breathe, let alone speak. In a few quick movements, the lacy bralette joined the pile of clothes and she was naked in front of me.

A roaring filled my ears and I gave up trying to make her see reason and reached for her instead. I'd been crazy since the moment I saw her, what was wrong with succumbing to the madness a little longer?

Her nimble fingers undid the catch on my jeans and

lowered the zipper. All I could do was hold onto her hips. Somehow the student had become the teacher. Her hands found me aching and hard as steel. She bent her knees, but I stopped her.

"No, c'mere." I guided her onto my lap and hissed at the meeting of heated flesh. "This way."

Layla made a sound in the back of her throat as she threw her head back and began working herself onto my cock. She wasn't completely wet, but the friction was glorious. Her thighs trembled as she lifted and seated herself until she engulfed me completely.

"You feel so good inside me," she whispered against the shell of my ear. "I just wanted to feel it one more time."

"Whatever you want," I answered.

Her hips already moved of their own accord. This was something past seduction, past attraction. All I wanted was to rear up and take her, make her mine, but I gripped her hips and let her do the taking. The were incredible pleasure in the submission.

She folded her legs, hooking her feet on the seat behind me until she found an angle that made her cry out and her hips buck wildly. Once, the students in the hallway beyond my door shouted, making her pace stumble. At first, I thought it frightened her, and maybe it did, but it also made her slick around me.

"Better be quiet, Layla. They may be able to hear you." Her strangled breathing filled my ears and the fingers gripping my arms would no undoubtedly leave bruises. "That lock isn't strong. If someone wanted to get in here they could. It would only take one hard push." She buried her face in my neck and her hips slowed as she tried to control herself. Not a chance. I gripped her hips and resumed the pace. She held onto me for dear life. "They're right there on the other side of the door. Less than five feet away. We're practically surrounded by people."

"Stop, someone might hear us."

"Do you really want me to? You feel so hot and wet around me, Lay. I want to feel you come on me one more time. I want to watch you when you do. Just make sure you don't make a sound." As though to punctuate my words, someone thudded against my office door and laughter burst out.

It shocked Layla so thoroughly, she nearly shot right off my lap. "It's okay," I said in her ear. "They haven't heard you yet. Come on me, Lay or I'll make you scream so loud the whole building will hear you."

"You're crazy," she panted, but her hips were dancing back and forth like mad. "We're going to get caught."

I got to my feet with her in my lap and her legs twitched around me and she slapped at my chest. "What are you doing?" she whisper-screeched. "Dash, no."

I flicked off the lights so the most anyone would see through the frosted glass were the hint of shadows. Beyond, bodies moved in the hallway, illuminated by the fluorescent glare from the lights above. It gave the illusion that we were in a room full of people.

"This is so wrong," she said as I pinned her back against the glass. She threw her head back when I lifted her legs over my forearms, and then sucked in a deep breath through her nose. "So wrong."

Her hands gripped my shoulder as I moved in and out of her. She couldn't move, couldn't do anything but take it. Her eyes rolled back behind her lids and she bit her lip so hard it appeared to be bloodless.

"So wrong, but it feels so good, doesn't it?" I said against her throat.

"I hate you," she answered. "Harder."

"Can't," I responded. "Someone might hear. They're so close if we make too much noise, they could hear you."

She sobbed against me, her hips arching to find the angle that would take her to completion, but I held her steady, kept my thrusts paced at the border of being agonizingly slow. She slapped at me until I pinned her arms, too.

"You're...such...a...jerk," Layla said in between pants.

As though to block me out, she turned her head to the side, which made me smile, though she couldn't see it. She was too busy looking at the shadows of the people on the other side of the window. The walls of her pussy clamped around me, and I hissed out a breath.

"Oh, God," she whispered.

Her back arched and I used my weight to press her more firmly against the unforgiving wood. "Better not make a sound," I said again.

"Oh, God, oh God, ohGod."

There was nothing like watching her come. Nothing in the world that compared, but I was willing to repeat it a thousand times, a million, to prove myself wrong. It was like watching a storm. Her face clouded over with concentration, the build of the orgasm rumbling just beneath the surface. Then her body drew up tight, her nipples contracted in to hard points, and her mouth opened to a wide oh of surprise. The calm. She would hold the sweet tension for a few moments suspended in time, then, like thunder and lighting all at once, she'd shake and explode over and around me. Then her muscles would melt, and her body would cover me like soft rain.

Yeah, I could see her come a million times and I'd never get used to it.

I'd always want to make her do it a million more.

CHAPTER NINETEEN

LAYLA

CHARLIE WAS STUCK on a double shift, but made us promise to tell her everything the following day. I couldn't wait for advice, so I invited Ember over to my apartment once the twins were down for the night. She came wearing a pair of yoga pants and a thin sweater over a camisole. In her hands she carried a baby monitor and a bottle of wine.

"I should have an hour or two before one of them wakes up wanting something and that should be enough time for us to kill this wine. Do you have any glasses?"

I was already pulling a bottle out of the cabinet. "Here."

She poured two healthy servings and handed me one. She lifted hers to mine and clinked. "To seeing the end in sight. Graduation can't come any sooner."

"I'll drink to that." The white wine was cool and crisp and just what I needed. It had been a long couple of days.

Ember pulled me to the couch, sat the baby monitor on the

coffee table, and tucked her feet beneath her. "Do I have to pull it out of you or are you going to tell me what's been going on?"

I cupped my wine glass in my palms and studied the liquid inside while I spilled the whole story about what had happened between me and Dash. Eyes bright, Ember listened intently, pausing me only to ask questions or emit shocked gasps. When I finished, she squealed and gripped my hand.

"Lay, I can't believe you've been keeping this a secret. Well, not a good one, because Charlie and I guessed something was going on between you two, I mean no one fights that much and doesn't end up in bed."

I winced. "Well, I hope no one else figured it out. We've been trying to keep a low profile so neither of us gets hurt. But that isn't what I wanted to talk to you about."

Ember took a long sip from her wine and settled more deeply into the couch. "I shouldn't be so excited because you've clearly been through the wringer, but I've been hip deep in calls. Both the girls just got over the flu so I need the distraction of someone else's life."

I pressed a hand to her knee. "Feel free to indulge in my drama. No judgement. Anyway, so after Dash took me out on the date, he dropped me off at home and who do I run into but his grandmother."

"No."

Nodding emphatically, I said, "Yes. I invited her inside and she sat down on this couch all regal like and warned me away from Dash like this was some soap opera from a million years ago and they're a royal family, which would make me the lowly peasant."

Ember drank deeply, wiped at her lips. "What did you say?"

"I didn't have time to say much of anything. She left before I could even put up an argument, but I was fuming."

"I'll bet you were. Did you tell Dash?"

I shook my head. "I couldn't. He loves his grandparents. He'd be devastated if I told him they were capable of doing something like this. Besides, it'd be my word against hers. He wouldn't believe me."

Ember didn't seem convinced. "I don't know. From what you've said, he seems to be pretty into you. I think you should tell him what's going on that way you can work through it together."

"Is that how you and Chris work through your problems?" I was still worried about her. She seemed pretty broken up about how he'd been treating her.

She nodded, then stopped herself. "I mean, it used to be. When things were good we could talk through anything. That's what makes a relationship work more than all of the other stuff. Communication. But this isn't about me and Chris. What happened after you talked to his grandmother? The miserable old hag," she added with another sip of wine.

"Well, I thought about everything for a long time, even though I'd already made up my mind once she tried to convince me otherwise."

"You always have to think things to death," Ember commented.

"I can't help it. I want to make sure I'm making the right choice."

"What did you decide?" she asked. "What did you tell Dash?" There was an edge of impatience in her town that made me smile.

"I decided that it would be best if we didn't see each other."

Ember deflated a little, composed herself before answering. "Oh, I guess I understand that. He is your T.A. and you fight like cats and dogs."

I held up a finger. "That's not all. I decided it would be best if we didn't see each other...until after the semester. That way neither of us gets in trouble. It'll also give us time to think about things and make sure this is actually something we want to do."

"You can't think yourself out of love," Ember said and that gave me pause.

"I'm not," but I drank deeply of my own wine. "I want us both to be sensible."

"There is no making sense of it. It happens when it happens. With the right person, there is no right timing."

Ignoring her, I said, "That's my point. If it's right, then it'll work out--after the semester is over."

"So you're going to let the old hag win?" Ember demanded.

"I'm not letting her win. I don't want her to have any ammo, that's all. Once I'm not in his class anymore she won't have any leverage over me or him. The last thing I'd want to do is risk his career. That's what's most important to me."

"I do understand that, I just think you're trying to control a situation that's uncontrollable."

"I'm not trying to control it. Let's call it stacking the deck in my favor," I amended.

Ember got up from the couch and retrieved the wine from the fridge. After topping off both of our glasses, she said, "Call it whatever you want, but it's still the same thing."

"I don't think so."

"What are you going to do about your mother?"

The buzz from the wine washed away all of my worries. "Why does she have to know?"

Ember clinked her glass against mine. "That's my girl."

* * *

THE APARTMENT WAS quiet after Ember left a couple hours later. I ached to go upstairs to Dash's room, could practically feel him despite the floors that separated us, but I knew the separation was for the best. I lay on the couch, still buzzed from the wine and randomly flipping through Netflix trying to find something to watch when my phone buzzed on the table beside me.

Noticing my mother's name on the screen, I hit ignore and let it ring to voicemail. I'd pay for it later, I was sure, but I didn't want to talk to her. Especially not when the scent of Dash's grandmother's perfume still lingered on the air. I'd had enough of controlling women for at least a week. Besides, all she was going to do I was complain that I hadn't reached out about the finance thing and I really wasn't interested. The closer it got to graduation, the less inclined I was to have anything to do with her plans for me.

I settled on some mindless piece of fluff to distract me from worrying about how bad her meltdown would be when I heard from her next. I'd switched my wine for a ginger ale and sipped as I let my mind wander. Inevitably, it settled on Dash, more specifically, on the encounter in his office.

I couldn't believe I let him do that to me. Couldn't believe the girl who had always confessed not only to hate his guts, but was a self-proclaimed rule-follower had not only let him do it, but had enjoyed it. It gave me a little quickening low in my belly every time I thought of how close we'd come to getting caught. And I'd liked it. I'd never come so hard and even now I could feel him inside me. I could remember the excitement and fear of having someone just on the other side of the thin barrier. Plus it was Dash. Fighting against him, feeling the edge of frustration heightened everything.

From the satisfied grin when I could open my eyes again, he knew exactly what I was thinking. Perhaps it had been punishment for teasing him, but it had been worth it. He'd had the upper hand for so long it was nice to be on top so to speak.

When my phone rang again, it took me a second to pull myself from the fantasy. One of these days, he'd let me be the dominant one. Even if he took some convincing, I figured it'd be fun to take our arguing to the bedroom. Maybe the way we clashed was the reason why it felt so explosive with him.

I almost let the phone go to my voicemail again, but something had me glancing at the screen out of habit. Training from my mother, no doubt. But it wasn't her name on the screen. It was Dash's.

"Hello?" I said, hoping my voice didn't sound as desperate as I thought.

His didn't sound breathless at all. It was smooth, confident, and the very same as the one that had been haunting my dreams. "Hey, sweetheart."

That's it. That's all he had to say for me to be right back in his dark office, naked and needy. I swallowed hard.

"You shouldn't be calling me."

Dash chuckled. I remembered how his eyes lit up when he laughed. I ached to see him, to watch that light appear. "This isn't the CIA. They aren't going to track our phone calls."

"What do you want?" I asked.

"I guess phone sex is a no-go?"

My blood heated. "Not funny. Is that why you called?" Just hearing him was enough to have me shifting restlessly on the couch. His voice was like an activator switch. My skin itched to feel his hands. My mouth yearned for his lips.

"No, but if you're ever lonely in the next three months, I'd be happy to serve as your own personal 1-900 number. Just say the word."

"I'm hanging up now," I warned. More to stop myself from begging than from actual irritation.

"You're no fun. I wanted to call to give you a head's up. The woman who was at the benefit will be at a gala my grandparents are a part of. I'm escorting her, but I didn't want you to think it was a date or anything."

I remembered her. Sleek and elegant. The kind of woman his grandmother would be ecstatic for him to be involved with. "Oh?" I said, because what do you say to that?

"If you want me to tell her no, I will. She saw you coming out of my office a while back and I didn't want her to be suspicious. Since we're laying low for another couple months, I thought this would be a good time to disprove her suspicions, at least for now. I didn't want you to be caught off guard if it got back to you. I want to be completely honest with you, Lay. That's how much I want this to work."

I muted the T.V. so I could think. When I didn't speak right away, Dash pressed, "Sweetheart? Say something. I'll do whatever you want me to here."

"I'm not happy, but I understand why you'd do it. As long as it's platonic, like you say, then I guess I'm fine with it. I don't want to put you in an awkward position, and I know how much your family means to you."

That and he had reason to be suspicious about his family. Knowing what his grandmother thought, and his feelings about honesty made the wine sour in my stomach. I wanted to tell him right then, but I was afraid of how he would handle it. My mother had chosen people over me my whole life. He was very close to his grandparents. Would he choose them over me, too?

I wasn't ready to know the answer.

Not yet, anyway.

"Are you sure? Say the word and I'll tell them no."

I swallowed back the sour taste in my throat. "I'm sure. I trust you. Besides, we're both going to be busy these next few weeks. I don't want you to think you have to check with me about plans. I appreciate it, but you don't owe me anything. Not until after the semester."

"Don't be stupid," he said without heat. "As far as I'm concerned this is the real thing. I'll check with you about anything that I feel will make you uncomfortable. You're important to me, Lay."

"You're important to me, too," I said, my chest flooding with emotion. "But we can't talk like this all the time. It makes it harder."

"Don't worry, sweetheart. You'll be back to arguing with me in no time. Especially when you consider that I'm giving your last paper a B."

With that, the line went dead and I stared at the phone, steaming.

Like hell that paper deserved a B.

I couldn't wait until I could punish him properly.

CHAPTER TWENTY

DASH

I KNEW the moment we walked into the ballroom and I saw Jessica standing in a sleek black gown waiting for me it was a terrible idea to agree to go with her. My grandmother clutched my arm and propelled me forward. Sometimes I was sure she thought I was sixteen instead of an adult.

"There are the Martin's," she said with barely disguised glee. "Let's go tell them hello."

Jessica beamed as we crossed the room to their side. I couldn't help but remember the calculating gleam in her eye when she'd confronted me in my office. She latched onto my arm the moment we got close.

"Dash, I'm so glad you could make it."

I removed her talons and forced a smile. "Thank you for inviting me."

She followed my grandparents and her parents to our assigned table. As we walked, she chattered on about the gala, but honestly it went in one ear and out the other. All I wanted was to find a way to escape. Being with her felt wrong down to the bone.

It was going to be a very long night.

I reached for a glass of champagne from a passing waiter along the way and drank deeply. As I was lowering the glass, a couple making their way across the room caught my attention. I sprung to my feet and in three long strides had my arms around the woman of the pair and smiled at the man.

"Mom, Dad. What are you two doing here? I thought you were in Washington."

My mother, Naomi Hampton, barely reached my shoulders. Her strawberry-blonde hair fell in sheets to the middle of her back, a rose-gold waterfall. Green eyes, the same shade as mine peered back at me, alight with excitement. A weight I didn't know I'd been carrying since I said goodbye to Layla, lightened.

I looked to my father, Peter Hampton, as he spoke, "The holidays are coming up. We thought we'd surprise you. Besides, mom mentioned you'd met someone and your mother couldn't contain herself at the thought."

Dad was about my height with dark brown eyes and the same dark hair as mine. Aside from my eyes, I inherited everything else from my father. Mom used to harass me about being his twin after the burden of carrying and delivering me..

I started to mention that Layla wasn't here, but caught myself before I could. Manners ingrained in me since childhood allowed me to introduce Jessica Martin to them without faltering. I guess I'd inherited my father's ease for smoothing over social situations, because no one seemed to notice my pause. Mom looked at me with interest, but that was probably because it had been a while since she'd seen me.

"Peter," Grandmother ordered after the introductions, "come sit. We have to catch up. They're about to serve dinner."

Dutifully, my father took the seat next to her, my mother on the opposite side. I sat next to Mom and Jessica took he open seat to my left.

Drinks were ordered, small talk made. Having my parents in attendance made the conversation much less stilted. I began to think the night might not be so bad after all.

Until the topic changed to my work and my plans after graduation.

"How is teaching going, Dash? Last I heard you were assigned a business class?"

I felt Jessica tense beside me, even though my gaze was on my mother. "It's going well. We're halfway through the semester and I haven't had any issues. Professor Johnson seems pleased."

"I'm happy to hear that, honey," Mom says, patting my arm.

"He's excited to join your campaign in the new year," Grandmother broke in. "I can't wait for the Hampton line to continue. I'm so proud."

I took a sip of my champagne before I responded. "Well, don't get too riled up about it. I haven't decided whether or not I'm going to join him."

Grandmother waved that away. "Don't be silly Dashiel. Of course you will."

Dad and I shared a look. He'd told me stories about how his

mother had pushed him, first into graduating at the top of his class, then into law school after college. Then up the ladder in politics. There hadn't been a moment in his life she didn't orchestrate, at least not until he met my mom. She was the one thing he chose without Grandmother's influence—which, according to family history, she hadn't been thrilled about. My mother hadn't come from a wealthy family. Her parents had been thoroughly middle class working people, good people, from what I've been told. They both passed away when I was young.

I ignored Grandmother's comment, like I ignored most of her behavior. She was my father's mother and deserved respect, but that didn't mean she was allowed to control my life the way she'd done his. He turned out alright, but that was only because he had Mom, or at least that's what he's told me several times over the years.

"Jessica, why don't we dance?" I suggested after we'd eaten.

Jessica beamed up at me and accepted my hand. I ignored the pleased look on my grandmother's face and led Jessica to the dance floor. She attached herself to me like a burr, but I reasoned it was only one dance. It'd give both of us some space from my family and I'd have an opportunity to set things straight.

"I love this song," she breathed into my ear.

I didn't even hear it. "Are you having a good time?" I asked politely.

Her claws contracted as thought to prevent as escape. "I'm having a wonderful time. Your grandparents are such wonderful people. I've been dying to meet your father. He's such an inspiration."

As she spoke, recounting the conversation at dinner, I couldn't help but think about Layla. She would have hated the gala, where most of the money went into throwing it than supporting the cause. I had a hard time She'd never be able to sit on the sidelines, blinded by the glitz and glamour. She'd want to be in the trenches, volunteering, organizing. She was a doer, not a watcher.

"Dash," Jessica prompted. "Did you hear me?"

"I'm sorry," I replied with a kind smile. "What were you saying?"

"I asked if you were having a nice time."

I nodded dispassionately. "Of course. Thank you again for coming."

Her eyes sharpened, and she cocked her head. The look reminded me so my much of my grandmothers that I blinked twice. "Are you sure? You don't even seem like you're here. Is something wrong?"

"No, of course not. I'm sorry. You've been wonderful, I'm afraid my heart's just not in it tonight." My only goal as far as she was concerned was to placate her suspicions.

Jessica's lips twisted. "It's that girl isn't it? That student? She's the one you're thinking about. Why you've been so distracted all night. Really, Dash? I thought you wanted me here because you'd given up on her."

I shook my head. "It's not about her. Or you. I didn't mean to lead you on, but you should know that I have no interest in pursuing a relationship with you. I'm sorry if that hurts your feelings, but—"

She cut me off before I could offer any more platitudes. "She is. You don't have to lie to me. I saw the way you looked at her when she left your office. I'm not stupid. I thought when you invited me here tonight that you'd come to your senses, but apparently not. I won't make a scene tonight, but you should really think about what you're doing. What you're risking. Is she worth it?"

The song ended and Jessica turned and glided back to our table. When she saw it was only my mother raining, she made a deft turn for the restrooms. That hadn't gone the way I'd expected. I hoped she meant what she said about not making a scene. Not for my sake, for Layla's.

Mom turned as she heard me approach and beamed when she saw me. "Good, you're father's gone schmoozing and I'm dying to hear more about what's been going on with you. I wish you'd come join us in Washington. I miss you."

"You sound like Grandmother," I said with a teasing smile.

"Blasphemy," she answered with a laugh. "You know better than to compare me with Elizabeth. Now, tell me all about this young lady you brought here tonight. Do you like her?"

"Jessica. She's nice, but it's not what you think."

"Oh," mom said with a tone of surprise. "Why not?"

I lifted a shoulder and sipped champagne that had gone warm. "I'm not interested in her romantically."

"So who is she?"

"Her parents are friends with grandmother and grandfather."

Mom laughed and her eyes twinkled. "I don't mean her, silly goose. I mean the girl you are interested in."

I sputtered slightly, choking on my drink. "What?"

"Don't play dumb. A mother knows when her son likes a woman. If it isn't this Jessica girl, then who is it?"

I thought of Layla with her obsession with books and her love of art. A woman who worked so hard to please everyone she sometimes forgot to please herself.

Mom slapped my shoulder affectionately. "I knew it. I told you. Who is she?"

"She's...complicated," I said slowly. "I'm still trying to figure it out. If something happens, you'd be the first to know, I promise."

"Well if she can put that look in your eye, I'd say you have it figured out," she teased. "But I'm patient. When it gets uncomplicated, you should bring her to meet us."

Jessica kept her word about not making a scene. At the end of the night, she'd managed to keep the conversation flowing and didn't say another word about the conversation we'd had on the dance floor. She left with her parents after thanking my grandparents and saying what a pleasure it was to meet my mom and dad. Being with someone like her would be so easy in this way. Her family was remarkably like mine. My grandmother certainly liked her.

The problem was she wasn't Layla. And she never would be.

It was as simple and as complicated as that. My parents took a car back to their hotel and my grandfather stayed behind to talk business with some contacts, which left me to drive my grandmother back home.

"That was a lovely evening," she said as she got into the passenger seat.

"It was. Did you have a nice time?" I asked.

"A lovely time. What did you think of Ms. Martin?" She was about as subtle as a rock.

"She seems great, but before you get any ideas, we're just friends. "

"Just friends? Is this a young person thing?"

"No, it's an I'm not interested in her kind of thing." I was thankful it would be a short drive.

Grandmother turned in her seat to face me with the same look in her eye she got when something went wrong in one of my father's carefully coordinated campaigns. "Don't be obtuse, Dashiel. She's a wonderful girl and the two of you make a beautiful suit."

"I'm sorry to disappoint you, grandmother, but it's not going to happen." I pulled into her driveway and unlocked the doors.

As I helped her out of her seat, she clasped my hands. "Why don't you take some time to think about it. She and her family will be attending Thanksgiving with us and you'll have more time to get to know one another." With that, she kissed me on the cheek and strode inside.

Now I know how my father must have felt his whole life. It

was no wonder he decided to move to Washington as soon as he could.

I gave a passing thought to calling Layla, but decided against it.

As I drove home, I thought of her and mentally calculated the days until I could see her again and make her mine for good.

CHAPTER TWENTY-ONE

LAYLA

"MS. TATE, Ms. Tate, there's a ghost!"

I smiled at the little boy who was working with pieces of magazine prints to recreate his own picture story as a part of an assignment for one of my education electives. "There's a ghost in your story?"

I would miss them when the class was over. I loved being in the classroom. Answering their questions. Watching a student exploring art was an experience without compare.

The little boy named Tony was a mischief maker, but he did well if he was encouraged to stay on task. He shook his dark brown curls and said, "No, Ms. Tate." Then, he pointed toward the classroom door. "Right there!"

I glanced over his shoulder, prepared to humor him, but found something more horror inducing than a ghost—Mrs. Hampton stood at the door, her pale overly made-up face peering through the keyhole window. I gasped before I could check my response, causing several other students to perk up from their assignments and follow my gaze to the door.

Mrs. Hampton knocked twice in rapid succession, then opened the door before I could get to my feet. She was as intimidating as ever. Not a hair was out of place and her outfit—a sleep, feminine suit--cost more than my entire wardrobe. She took a step inside, pausing by the door.

"Tony, why don't you finish up here while I talk with our visitor?" I replaced the glue I was using and got to my feet.

I trembled with a combination of humiliation and rage, but I tried my best not to let it show. Lifting a hand, I gestured to the hall. "Why don't we talk outside where there's more privacy?"

With a derisive little sniff, she turned on her heel and I followed her out into the hall.

"What are you doing here?" I asked when we were alone. The hallway was blessedly deserted. It was embarrassing enough being confronted by her again without having it witnessed by a colleague or student. "This is my job. You shouldn't be here."

"I wouldn't be here if you'd taken my advice from our last conversation."

"What I do or don't do in my personal life is none of your business."

"If it involves my family, it is my business." She reached into her leather bag, dug around, then pulled out a pocketbook. She flipped it open with easy, clearly used to spending money like it was water. The gold glint of her pen flashed in the dingy light from the fluorescents overhead. She scribbled in a neat scrawl on a blank check.

I took a step backward, uncomprehending. "I think you should leave," I sputtered before she could say a word. She wasn't doing what I thought she was. People only did that sort of things in the movies. There was no way this was real life. I glanced back at my classroom to find my students peeking up from their work to see what I was doing. At my glance, they turned their attention back to their desks.

"I'm afraid I can't do that," she said, still writing.

"Don't make me call security," I warned. How had she even gotten past the front desk? I didn't think she had any kids here at the school.

She gave a mirthless laugh and arched a perfect brow. "Please do," Mrs. Hampton invited. "My family has donated thousands of dollars to the public school system."

I gritted my teeth. It was like dealing with a steel wall. She should have gone into politics instead of her husband. People like her, and my mom, expected others to bow to their will. They saw the world as theirs for the ruling. A migrain pounded behind my eyes.

"Then what do you want?" I asked in a measured tone. The sooner I could get it out of her, the sooner I could make her leave. "Dash and I aren't together, so I'm not sure what you're doing here."

She ripped a check out of her checkbook and snapped it closed. After thrusting it back into her bag, she pursed her lips, then said, "I'm not an idiot, Ms. Tate. Dashiel may have brought Jessica to the gala last night, but a woman knows when a man isn't interested and his mind was on someone else."

I brushed my hair out of my face, wishing I could feel half as put together as she was. "I'm not sure what you want me to do about that. I can't control how someone feels." Which was an understatement.

She shoved the check under my nose. "That may be so, but you can make sure he has no reason to keep his hopes up."

I glanced at the check. I couldn't help it—it was practically down my throat. There were so many zeroes my eyes crossed. "Is this a joke?" I blurted out. "I'm not taking your money. Are you insane?" My voice rose with each word and I checked myself before someone else could hear.

"Think about it, Ms. Tate. This money could set you up for the next chapter of your life. You've only known Dashiel for a short time. Is that acquaintance worth passing up such an opportunity?"

Heat flamed across my cheeks and my eyes narrowed. I clenched my hands into fists at my sides. "You must think very little about your grandson," I said, my voice vibrating with fury.

"On the contrary," she said coolly, "I think very highly of my grandson." The disdain for me couldn't have been clearer. "I want what is best for him. I thought I'd been perfectly frank the first time around, but I should have considered you'd need a motivator."

"This conversation is over. I'll do you the favor of never speaking of this to Dash because it would break his heart, but let me make it clear: whatever I do with Dash is none of your business. I will never take your money. Now you need to leave."

She reached forward, but I was so angry I was frozen to the spot. With a quick movement, she tucked the check into the pocket of my khaki pants. "In case you change your mind." Mrs. Hampton put on a sleek pair of sunglasses, then stopped a few steps away. "I hope I've made myself clear. I wouldn't want something to happen with your education. It would be a shame."

With that parting shot, she waved her fingers in my direction and sauntered off.

I stayed by the door to my classroom. Less than five minutes had passed, but it felt like my whole world was off its center axis. Did that really just happen? It was a complete nightmare.

Before returning to my students, I took some time to calm my emotions. I couldn't let them see me upset. Even though I waited until my breathing calmed and my face cooled off, the moment I walked into the classroom and sat next to Tony, he turned his boyish face up and said, "Is everything okay, Ms. Tate? Do you want a candy? Candy always makes me feel better when I'm upset."

I ruffled his silken hair. "I'm fine, sweetheart. Just grown up stuff. Nothing to worry about. Why don't you show me what you were working on while I was gone?"

ALL I WANTED after my student teaching was done for the

day was an hour at the gym to clear my thoughts and a long, steaming hot shower. It had been hours since our confrontation, but I still felt like I was covered in a sticky, slimy residue. It was the same feeling I got after a family vacation with my mother for a week without an escape.

I went home to change into gym clothes and made my way back to campus. The gym was always packed with students, but the equipment was top-of-the-line and free for students, so it was worth the drive. I scanned my I.D. at the sensor and plugged in my headphones, hoping to drown out the booming music and buzz of conversation. All I wanted to do was disappear for a little while.

When I saw Charlie on the treadmill, I had to admit, I wasn't super stoked. I didn't want anyone to see me like this. Didn't want them to read the conflict in my eyes. But I couldn't turn away when she recognized me, brightened, and waved.

I crossed the crowded gym to her side and took out an earbud. "Hey! I didn't expect to see you here."

She bounded off the treadmill, her face pink with exertion. "Layla! I'm so happy to see you. It's been so busy at work I feel like it's been forever. I don't want to interrupt your workout, but I'd love to catch up with you. It's not the same nice I moved in with Liam."

I shook my head. "Of course. You finished here?" I asked.

"I've got about fifteen more minutes if you don't mind joining me?" She said.

"Sure." I wrapped my towel around the bar and stepped up to the treadmill beside hers. "How has work been?"

Charlie bumped up her speed and resumed her trot. "Hell, that's why I'm here. Liam got tired of listening to me complain, so he forced me to go to the gym a couple times a week to work off my frustrations."

"That bad, huh?" The brisk pace of my own treadmill caused me to pant a little.

She grimaced. "It's not bad, really. Just a lot of red tape and a lot to learn. I complain about it, but I'm loving it." Charlie shot me a look and swiped at her brow. "But that's not what we were going to talk about. Ember updated me about everything that was going on. I'm sorry I couldn't make it to the last pow wow."

"You don't have to apologize. I know you're busy. You don't have to drop everything for me."

Even though she was nearly jogging, Charlie still had energy enough to give me a look that said don't-be-stupid. "I'm not even going to touch on that. From what Ember said, you've had a lot on your plate, too. I just want to be there for you."

"You're always there for me."

"I hate to say this, but you looked like you got run over by a truck. Did something else happen? Do I need to kick Dash's ass? You say the word and I'll do it."

I laughed, but it was half-hearted. "Well, I'm assuming Ember told you about what his grandmother did a little while ago?"

"Yeah, the dusty old bitch. Oh my god, did she do something else?" She abruptly turned off her treadmill. "Let's do some weights. I need to be able to focus and I can't do that when I'm almost out of breath."

"It just happened," I said, following her. "I don't even know what to think."

"Well, spill. I'm happy to commiserate and say some chants to curse her for life. One of my patients in a witch and she's been teaching me some stuff."

Selecting a dumbbell, I sighed. "It's a long story."

"We have time. It'll help you feel better to talk about it. What happened?"

"Fine, but no curses. I don't need the bad karma."

Charlie did a few bicep curls. "I promise."

As we worked through several weight training exercises, I recounted the conversation with Elizabeth Hampton, getting more and more angry and desolate the second time around.

"You have to tell Dash!" Charlie said when I finished.

"I can't. Would you want to hear that?"

It was already bad enough that I hadn't mentioned the first conversation to him. The second would kill him. As much as this break was killing me, I was grateful for the time to process what had happened so I could figure out how to handle it.

"I would want to know if my family was scheming behind my back. So would he."

I reverse curled as I considered. "Maybe. I have some time to think about it while we're on this break until the end of the semester. You never know. Maybe he won't even want to get back together and it won't be an issue."

Charlie just shook her head. "You're being too pessimistic. We've all seen how Dash is around you. You've got it bad for him, too, and you know it. You're just too afraid to admit it to yourself."

"We don't even get along most of the time!" I blurted out. "We argue more often than not. Not to mention his grand-mother. There are so many things working against us."

"Then don't make a decision now. Take the break to think about it. But first, you've got to tell me... How much money was it?"

I couldn't help but laugh. "I'm not telling you that. No amount of money could have convinced me to walk away from him."

Charlie just smiled. "I guess that means you have your answer."

She reached forward, but I was so angry I couldn't move. With a quick movement, she tucked the check into the pocket of my khaki pants. "In case you change your mind." Mrs. Hampton put on a sleek pair of sunglasses and started to leave, then stopped a few steps away. "I hope I've made myself clear here. I wouldn't want something to happen with your educa-tion. It would be a shame."

With that parting shot, she waved her fingers in my direc-tion and sauntered off.

I stayed by the door to my classroom. Less than five minutes had passed, but it felt like my whole world was off it's center axis. Did that really just happen? It felt like a nightmare.

Before returning to my students, I took some time to calm my emotions. I couldn't let them see me upset. Even though I waited until my breathing calmed and my face cooled off, the moment I walked into the classroom and sat down next to Tony, he turned his boyish face up to me and said, "Is everything okay, Ms. Tate? Do you want a candy? Candy always makes me feel better when I'm upset."

I ruffled his silken hair. "I'm fine, sweetheart. Just grown up stuff. Nothing to worry about. Why don't you show me what you were working on while I was gone?"

* * *

ALL I WANTED after my student teaching was done for the day was an hour at the gym to clear my thoughts and a long, steaming hot shower. It had been hours since our confrontation, but I still felt like I was covered in a sticky, slimy residue. It was the same feeling I got after a family vacation with my mother for a week without an escape.

I went home to change into gym clothes and made my way back to campus. The gym was always packed with students, but the equipment was top-of-the-line and free for students, so it was worth the drive. I scanned my I.D. at the sensor and plugged in my headphones, hoping to drown out the booming music and buzz of conversation. All I wanted to do was disappear for a little while.

When I saw Charlie on the treadmill, I had to admit, I wasn't super stoked. I didn't want anyone to see me like this. Didn't want them to read the conflict in my eyes. But I couldn't turn away when she recognized me, brightened and waved.

I crossed the crowded gym to her side and took out an earbud. "Hey! I didn't expect to see you here."

She bounded off the treadmill, her face pink with exertion. "Layla! I'm so happy to see you. I've been so busy at work I feel like it's been forever. I don't want to interrupt your workout, but I'd love to catch up with you. It's not the same nice I moved in with Liam."

I shook my head. "Of course. You finished here?" I asked.

"I've got about fifteen more minutes if you don't mind joining me?" She said.

"Sure." I wrapped my towel around the bar and stepped up to the treadmill adjacent to hers. "How has work been?"

Charlie bumped up her speed and resumed her trot. "Hell, that's why I'm here. Liam got tired of listening to me complain, so he forced me to go to the gym a couple times a week to work off my frustrations."

"That bad, huh?" The brisk pace of my own treadmill caused me to pant a little.

She grimaced. "It's not bad, really. Just a lot of red tape and a lot to learn. I complain about it, but I'm loving it." Charlie shot me a look and swiped at her brow. "But that's not what we were going to talk about. Ember updated me about everything that was going on. I'm sorry I couldn't make it to the last pow wow."

"You don't have to apologize. I know you're busy. You don't have to drop everything for me."

Even though she was nearly jogging, Charlie still had energy enough to give me a look that said don't-be-stupid. "I'm not even going to touch on that. From what Ember said, you've had a lot on your plate. I just want to be there for you."

"You're always there for me, silly."

"I hate to say this, but you looked like you got run over by a truck. Did something else happen? Do I need to kick Dash's ass? You say the word and I'll do it."

I laughed, but it was half-hearted. "Well, I'm assuming Ember told you about what his grandmother did a little while ago."

"Yeah, the dusty old bitch. Oh my god, did she do something else?" She abruptly turned off her treadmill. "Let's do some weights. I need to be able to focus and I can't do that when I'm almost out of breath."

"It just happened," I said, following her. "I don't even know what to think."

"Well, spill. I'm happy to commiserate and say some chants to curse her for life. One of my patients in a witch and she's been teaching me some stuff."

Selecting a dumbbell, I sighed. "It's a long story."

"We have time. It'll help you feel better to talk about it. What happened?"

"Fine, but no curses. I don't need the bad karma."

Charlie did a few bicep curls. "I promise."

As we worked through several weight training exercises, I recounted the conversation with Elizabeth Hampton, getting more and more angry and desolate as time wore on.

"You have to tell Dash!" Charlie said when I finished.

"I can't. Would you want to hear that?"

It was already bad enough that I hadn't mentioned the first conversation to him. The second would kill him. As much as this break was killing me, I was grateful for the time to process what had happened so I could figure out how to handle it.

"I would want to know if my family was scheming behind my back. So would he."

I reverse curled as I considered. "Maybe. I have some time to think about it while we're on this break until the end of the semester. You never know. Maybe he won't even want to get back together, and it won't even be an issue."

Charlie just shook her head. "You're being too pessimistic. We've all seen how Dash is around you. You've got to know how he feels, or you never would have let this go so far. You've got it bad for him and you know it. You're just too afraid to admit it to yourself."

"We don't even get along most of the time!" I blurted out. "We argue more often than not. Not to mention his grand-mother. There are so many things working against us."

"Then don't make a decision now. Take the break to think about it. But first, you've got to tell me...How much money was it?"

I couldn't help but laugh. "I'm not telling you that. I will tell you that no amount of money could have convinced me to walk away from him."

Charlie just smiled. "I guess that means you have your answer."

CHAPTER TWENTY-TWO

DASH

I HAVE three missed calls from Jessica and three times as many text messages, but there's nothing from Layla. Not that I was expecting there to be. She made it clear that taking this break meant minimal to no contact and I understood.

That didn't mean I had to like it.

She would have killed me if I took a ride down to her apartment, even though I thought about doing just that dozens of times a day. My sleep was shit because all I could do was remember her in my bed and think about how impossibly close she was. Just an elevator ride away. In less time than it would take to order an espresso, I could have my hands on her, could have her body beneath mine.

The time between now and the end of the year seemed to multiply with each passing day.

I've kept our relationship as professional as possible, like she requested. I only saw her during class and never showed her any preferential treatment. She sat every Monday, Wednesday, and Friday in the same spot in the lecture hall. I made it a point not to stare, but I'd watch her out of the corner of my eye or whenever I gave a reading assignment or when the other students were distracted.

I began searching for her face in the crowds on campus. Even though there were thousands of students, I always seemed to think I recognized her everywhere. It drove me a little crazy.

Sighing, I got to my feet. It had been another sleepless night and, I'd needed about two pots of coffee in order to face the day. While it brewed, I took a shower and stroked myself under the hot spray thinking of Layla's face when she'd come in my office. There was something about pushing her to those limits. Watching her overcome the apprehension and dive into the pleasure without hesitation. I ached with the need to see her, touch her, taste her again. Hell, another one of our arguments would probably do it for me at this point.

The shower and jerking off didn't help. Thinking about her only made it worse. It had been less than a month since we agreed to take some space, another two were going to kill me.

I thought about visiting my parents for a distraction when I was finished with my own classes for the day, but decided against it. When they visited, it almost always ended with my grandmother barging in at some point and I really didn't want to be poked at anymore about what a nice girl Jessica was.

I poured the coffee into a thermos and dressed in loose gym shorts and a light long-sleeved shirt. I had a couple hours before I needed to be in class and a long, exhausting walk sounded like the best way to spend it. As I was locking up, the elevator dinged and drew my eye. Cursing. I jogged to it hoping to reach it before it shut again.

"Hey, man," Tripp said as I walked into the elevator. He had a bag slung over his shoulder and was wearing a similar getup, track pants and a light long-sleeved shirt.

Relieved at seeing a familiar face, I said, "Hey, what are you doing up so early?"

Tripp also lived in the building and hung out sometimes during Taco Tuesdays with Ember. An idiot could tell he had a thing for her, but both of them tried to say they were just friends. Not my business.

He adjusted the bag over his shoulder. "Practice, dude. I've got gym for an hour this morning for weight trainIng, then some team drills."

"It's not even season yet and you have to get up this early to practice?" Sports outside of recreational football, had never really been my thing.

"Year-round, dude. Baseball is life. Where are you going this early?" He asked as we got off the elevator at the parking garage.

I waved my thermos of coffee around. "I thought about heading out to do some working out of my own."

"Why don't you ride with me to the gym?"

"Are you sure, man? I don't want to get in your way."

"Don't worry about it. It's free training in the off season, so the other guys won't care. We can throw some balls around. Whatever."

"Sure, why not?" I could use the distraction.

NICOLE BLANCHARD

"We can take my car. I'll drop you back by here after the gym."

Tripp lead me to a beat up old Honda Civic. For some reason, it wasn't the sort of car I imagined the star baseball player would drive, but I didn't comment.

"Haven't seen you around Taco Tuesdays lately," Tripp said as we buckled up.

I shrugged. "I figured I'd give Layla some room."

"Did the two of you have another fight?"

The teasing tone in his voice made me smile a little for the first time in a while. "I guess we aren't very subtle."

"About as subtle as a foul ball to the back of your head."

"We're just taking some space. It's hard being objective when she's one of my students. She takes her education very seriously."

"Ahh, I get it," Tripp said with a sly glance in my direction.

"Get what?"

"You've got a thing for her, right?"

"That obvious?"

Tripp drove lazily with one hand on the wheel and the other on his thigh. I'd never given him much consideration to him before now because I'd been so focused on Layla, but he wasn't all that bad. I didn't normally hang out with the jock types, but he wasn't in your face about it. In fact, he seemed pretty down to earth.

"Nah, I overheard Ember talking to Charlie about it the other day when we were studying."

"Oh, studying. Right. Is that what the kids call it now?"

214

"It's okay, I won't say you're projecting. And I won't tell Lay you've been pining over her."

"You mean like no one has ever told Ember you're into her, too?"

Tripp grinned, surprising me. "That's old news, man. I asked her out once freshman year, but I was a bit of a manwhore back then and she didn't take me seriously. Blew my chance. Then she hooked up with Chris and the rest is history. We're just friends now."

"You do know she and Chris have been arguing, right?"

"They always argue. Get back together. It's a two person soap opera."

"So why do you stick around? Star baseball player, self-proclaimed ladies man and all. Do you enjoy watching her with her boyfriend or something? No judgement if you do, I know some people are into that."

"No worse than you getting off on picking fights with Layla." At my less than amused look, Tripp laughed. "Like I said, we're just friends."

"If you say so."

* * *

AFTER CLASS A FEW WEEKS LATER, I pack up my things with lightning speed. It's the only way I've managed to keep myself from watching Layla leave and not feel like a fucking stalker. As a result, my work has never been better, even my grandmother seemed pleased by my participation in planning my father's upcoming year during the recent Thanksgiving break to pass the time. Begrudgingly, I even happened to enjoy it, not that I told her. She would have taken that news and run with it.

Jessica's texts had slowed down to one a day. Despite our conversation at the gala, she still didn't seem t understand that I wasn't going to be interested. I wasn't sure why she didn't just give it up, but I had other things on my mind.

Which is why, when I look up and find Layla standing next front of me waiting patiently, I frose, unsure of what to do. That's what she's done to me. Turned me into a man who is so completely rocked by a woman, he didn't know which way was up. I could only stare at her as the classroom emptied, leaving us alone.

"Do you have a second?" she asked.

Fuck me, but her voice had me instantly, painfully hard. I'd missed it. I'd deliberately not called on her in class so I wouldn't have to listen to her answer a question. I wasn't sure I could have hidden my response. For this exact reason.

"I don't think that's a good idea," I answered and edged toward the exit. "If you have any questions about the material, you can email them to me, and I'll answer them as soon as possible."

"Dash," she said softly. "Please."

Her hair was up in a messy bun.. She wore a slightly wrinkled FSU hoodie and skinny jeans. Her face was bare of makeup and there were dark smudges under her eyes, like she hadn't been sleeping well.

"What's wrong?" I asked. "Are you okay?"

"Can we talk in your office?" she asked instead of answering.

Considering what had happened there the last time, I wavered before saying, "Sure, of course. I've got a few minutes."

As we walked the short distance, I wondered what the hell made her change her mind about keeping her distance. Then, I worried maybe she'd already made a decision.

I unlocked the door to my office and led her inside, making sure to keep a respectful distance. She sat in the visitor chair at my desk, but I remained standing. My desk chair drew to mind too many erotic visions of her on my lap. I needed to keep a clear mind.

"What's going on?" I asked to fill the silence.

She got back to her feet and began to pace. "I've been thinking about this for a long time and I don't exactly know where to start."

Much as I wanted to tell her to cut the shit and spit it out, I kept silent as she fidgeted and paced.

"I guess I should start at the beginning." She spun around and her eyes flashed. "You're a jerk."

My brows lifted. That certainly wasn't what I was expecting her to say.

"You're a jerk. And you drive me crazy more often than not. I know we spend just as much time arguing as we do having regular conversation. I've never been good at the relationship thing, it's why I've been single most of my life and why I was a virgin at twenty-two. I've never met a man who made me want to stop being alone. It's safe that way. I know what to expect, how to be. I'm used to control. If my mother isn't dictating how my life should be, then I'm planning every second to death so I'm not caught off guard."

Her hands fisted at her side, she looked a bit like an avenging angel. "But I didn't plan you. You were unexpected. Every minute I'm with you I feel alive. Being with you makes me feel explosive. And it was scary at first how strong those feelings were. And a part of me hated that you were the one who caused them."

I opened my mouth to protest, but she shot me a look that had me slamming it shut again.

"Aside from Ember and Charlie, you are the only other person in my life who takes my thoughts and dreams and opinions seriously. I think you push me because you know it's the only time I show you the real me instead of the person programmed to mimic the viewpoints of everyone else around me."

She took a step closer, her hands coming to my chest. My whole body was wire-tight. "You're a jerk," she said softly, " but I love you, anyway."

Then she kissed me. I was so stunned, all I could do was hold on.

She tasted like salvation, and I was a sinner of the worst sort.

Then my office door flew open and Jessica stood in the doorway behind a gaping Professor Michaels.

CHAPTER TWENTY-THREE

LAYLA

I DON'T KNOW what Dash said to his boss as I waited in the hallway next to the smirking woman. She was lucky I never resorted to physical violence because I'd never wanted to deck someone so much in my life.

But I knew it wasn't really her fault. Spiteful bitch she may be, but I'd made the choice to see him. If anyway was going to be punished here it should be me.

There hadn't been a pause for me to speak with Dash, to decide what our story was, how we were going to protect not only my standing in his class, but his job, too. His reputation.

There hadn't been a moment for me to apologize. This was all my fault. His grandmother had been right about that. If I'd kept my mouth shut, stayed away, none of this would be happening. Part of me knew that wasn't true, but the part that was still the vulnerable girl at graduation was afraid she was right.

Speaking of his grandmother, I still hadn't told him about what happened. How had everything spiraled so fantastically out of control?

I thought I'd been doing the right think by risking it all and letting him know how I felt.

The thing with risking it all is that you have to be willing to make the gamble...and lose.

I chewed on my thumbnail and watched the shadows on the other side of the misted glass moving around. Above the din of the students milling around the hallway and the riotous conversation, I could hear the professors raised voice and Dash's calm, soothing baritone.

Had it been worth it?

I could hear my mother's snotty voice in my head, judging me, criticizing as she often did. She'd find out soon enough, but I already knew what she was going to say. That I'd been stupid to bet everything on a man. That my future was worth more than any man, that none of them could be trusted, and I was just like every other idiot girl who gave up her life for a roll in the sheets.

For so long I'd listened to her dictate like she knew what she was talking about. But one thing I'd realized about growing up was that if there was a universal truth it was that no one knew what they were doing. We were all like balls in an arcade game crashing around, pinging off the walls hoping we'd win, but not really knowing how.

God, I guess I was more like her than I thought possible. I tried to control everyone in my little circle as though it had any bearing on the outcome. In my effort to control my relationship with Dash to circumvent getting caught, what had happened?

We'd been caught.

I used to think nothing was worth throwing away my future. Like a bull, I kept my head down, forging a path from grade school to graduation, not letting anything stop me. Stubborn, as Dash would say. Until now, I would have argued with him, naturally, but deep down, I would have known he was right. Like he'd been right about so many things.

The door opened and I straightened, the breath immediately wheezing out of my chest at the sight of Dash appearing in the doorway. Jessica straightened too, and while she'd looked bored and smug while we'd waited, her face brightened when he walked out. He didn't even spare her a glance, which caused her to deflate.

Professor Michaels, a stern man in his mid-fifties with a white fluff of hair and immaculately trimmed goatee, hovered in the doorway. He didn't say anything when Dash came to my side, but there was a disapproving frown on his lips.

That didn't bode well.

"Let's get out of here," Dash said, and took my hand.

We left Jessica and the professor staring after us—or at least, I thought we did.

I didn't look back to find out.

DASH DIDN'T SPEAK ALL the way back to the apartment. I

was too dumbstruck to say anything. My hands were clammy and knotted in my lap the whole drive. Fear clawed at my throat, and a cold sweat dripped down my spine.

The elevator ride up to my floor was silent. Dash seemed to vibrate with tension. I wasn't sure if he was dropping me off and never going to speak to me again, or if he was just waiting until we had some privacy before giving me a thorough tongue lashing. I almost wished he would. Part of me felt like I deserved it.

My hands trembled as I unlocked my door and let him inside. It felt like years had passed since we spoke in his office when, after confirming with a glance at the clock on my microwave, it had been a little over an hour.

"Can I use your bathroom?" Dash asked when he'd stepped inside behind me.

"O-of course."

I pushed my hands through my hair and made my way to the kitchen to make some coffee to give myself something to do to keep busy. As I was pouring two mugs, Dash appeared in the hallway. I froze with the mugs in my hands.

God, why did he have to be so beautiful?

It really wasn't fair.

His hair was slightly messy where he must have run his hands through it a thousand times. He tended to do that when he was deep in thought. His brilliant green eyes were bloodshot, probably from the stress and rubbing them too much. Maybe he was having as much trouble sleeping as I was. He wore a flannel shirt tucked into dark jeans, but he'd missed a button somewhere so it was slightly lopsided, which made me smile. Even that little imperfection didn't take away from how good he looked.

"Coffee?" I asked when the moment stretched on too long.

He nodded. "Thanks."

We sipped in silence until he sighed. "What a day."

"I'll say," I murmured, then mustered up my nerve. "Did he fire you?"

Dash didn't seem shocked by my question. He merely sipped his coffee as he gathered his thoughts. "I'm not sure yet. There's going to be some sort of informal investigation. They're going to interview a couple people, check our correspondence on the university email, your grades and all that to see if you were given any sort of preferential treatment. They'll probably call you for an interview, too, to make sure I didn't coerce or intimidate you into giving me sexual favor in return for better grades."

I sputtered into my coffee. "Well, I guess they have to be fair. I should have thought of that, though." That made Dash smile, but I still felt lousy. "I'm sorry. I never should have come to you today. It was a bad move on my part. If I'd kept to the plan, none of this would have happened."

Dash sat his empty cup on the countertop and pulled me into his arms. "I'm glad you did. I was dying not talking to you. Fuck the consequences. We'll deal with them."

I yawned into his chest, soothed by the warm, musky scent of him. "I know we need to talk about this and there's a lot I still have to say, but I'm pretty worn out and I haven't slept good since I stayed the night here. What do you think about a nap?"

"I'd say you're speaking my language."

* * *

I KNEW it wouldn't take my mother long to stick her nose in my business. I wasn't surprised when, later that night, she knocked twice at my door before inserting the key I certainly didn't authorize her to have, and barreling through looking like an Amazon on a mission. Thank god we were both dressed and had fallen asleep on the couch after our short conversation.

"Mom!" I exclaimed as we sat up. Dash stayed close with a hand protectively on my waist. "How did you get in?"

She glared at the space between Dash and I before saying, "I have a key. Are you going to explain why I received a call from Elizabeth Hampton asking me to control my daughter?"

My face burned. "Why do you have a key to my apartment?"

Mom dismissed my words with a flick of her handbag and scoffed. "I pay for this apartment, in case you've forgotten. Of course I have a key."

"Mom, you can't just burst in here like this. You may be paying for the apartment, but it's my house. You could at least call before you came over."

"Layla Lucille you do not talk to me like that. I knew there was something going on. You haven't been yourself for months. First it was the internship, then it was dodging my calls. It's because of this boy, isn't it?"

"Mrs. Tate, Layla is a great girl she—"

Mom looked at him with a freezing glare that could have flayed skin with it's intensity alone. "Don't you tell me about my daughter. Everything was going on just fine until you came along and preyed on her. You should be ashamed of yourself. If your grandmother hadn't already reported you to the Dean, I would have done it myself."

I jumped to my feet. "He didn't prey on me, Mom. In case you've forgotten, I've known Dash my whole life. If anyone preyed on anyone, I preyed on him."

"Don't be ridiculous. I know what his kind is like. Men with power who target young, innocent girls. Your father was the same way, and I refuse to let it happen to you."

"It's not up to you, Mom. Not every man is like Dad. I'm not going to make the same mistakes you made. I'm going to make new ones. Big ones. But it's my life. I should be allowed to make them. I'm tired of you thinking you can control everything about me down to the career I pick."

"Not this again. I'm just trying to do what's best for you. Teachers make peanuts. Finance is a stable career."

"I don't want to talk about this anymore. I'd like you to leave."

Mom looked like I'd slapped her. "You can't be serious."

"I think we'll talk about this when you're ready to have a mature conversation and treat me like an adult. That includes requesting to speak to me, not barging into my house. It means treating my opinions and desires as equally important. I'm not yours to treat like a puppet, Mom. I'm a person with my own dreams. My own visions for my life. If you can't respect that, then maybe we need to reevaluate our relationship."

There was a long tense silence. Mom's shoulders heaved as she breathed heavily. Her eyes were bright with a fury I'd never seen before. Then again, I'd never stood up to her before, either. For a moment I was afraid she was going to throw a tantrum like a toddler right there in my living room, but she merely shouldered her bag and gave me a disdainful look. "You are making a mistake. The difference is that I won't be there to correct it when it blows up in your face."

"I'm sorry you feel that way," I said to her retreating back.

"Not as sorry as I am," she said. She took two steps through the doorway, paused, and then turned back. My heart fell to my feet. I braced before she spoke in a low, guttural voice. "I always knew you were a stupid girl, but I tried my hardest to do what I could to make you successful in this world. I gave you every opportunity and in return, you practically spit them back in my face. When I heard Elizabeth Hampton offered you a fortune to walk away for this boy, I thought 'Finally, Layla will see some sense.' Money like that would have taken you much farther than a man ever could. But no. You were too stupid to know a good thing when it hit you in the face."

With that little bomb deployed, she spun around and disappeared through the door.

CHAPTER TWENTY-FOUR

DASH

IT TOOK a few heart-rending moments for the gravity of Layla's mother's words to penetrate. *Offered you a fortune* kept repeating in my head like a battle cry. My grandmother, my family, bribed Layla. I should have been surprised, but the only emotion I could muster was disappointment, which battled with a numbness I couldn't quite shake.

I couldn't look at Layla while the information sank in, afraid to see the expression on her face. Was it true? One glance at her would tell me the answer.

But I didn't even need that.

Her silence told me everything I needed to know.

When I found my voice, I asked, "Is it true?" while staring at the plush rug beneath my feet. My head felt too heavy for my neck to lift. "Is what your mother said—is it true?"

Layla's sniffles were an arrow straight to my heart, but I held myself away from her, afraid if I looked, I'd shatter. After a moment, she sighed heavily, and said, "I was going to tell you."

I surged to my feet, but there was nowhere to go. I rounded on her. "Why didn't you tell me? When did this happen? What exactly did she say to you?"

She studied her feet, the top of her messy bun coming undone, tendrils of hair framing her ghost-white cheeks. "I didn't tell you because I knew it would hurt you. You love your family. I didn't want to be the one to break your heart. I thought, if we didn't work out it wouldn't matter anyway. You would never find out. If we did, then I'd cross that bridge when I figured out what I was going to do about us."

"When?" I demanded in a bark that caused her to flinch.

"After the gala, I think. She came to me when I was doing my student teaching and pulled me out of class." Layla shuddered as she spoke. It pissed me off that I was too angry to comfort her. It pissed me off that I wanted to comfort her. It pissed me off that so soon after she admitted how she felt, I was being confronted with this shit. "She told me that you deserved better and that if I knew what was good for me, I'd take the money and keep my mouth shut."

"Why would you tell me you loved me now?" I thought of all the women who'd chased me because of my family. The ones who'd only cared abou tmy money or my looks. Layla wasn't like that. She was headstrong, stubborn as an ox, and the smartest woman I knew. She wouldn't use me that way.

But there was an insidious fear inside of me that slithered and coiled like a snake. It whispered fuel into the doubts that sprang free. If your own family thought they could buy you future, why not the woman who cared about you?

At this, her head snapped up, eyes flashing like lightning. "Because I do love you."

It hurt to hear the words. If my own family could treat me like a commidty, what was stopping her from doing the same thing? "And yet you took the money. How much was I worth to you, Layla?"

My words shocked her to silence and she gaped at me, her previously pale cheeks flooding with color. She jumped to her feet snarling, "How could you ever think I would do something like that?"

"Are you saying you didn't?"

She glared and bared her teeth. "Of course not. What kind of person do you think I am?" She held up a hand to stop my answer. "You know what? Don't answer that. I think it would be insulting to both of us."

"Why didn't you tell me? Were you going to change your mind?" I don't know why I said it, don't know where the words came from, but they were out before I could take them back. It wasn't really her I was angry with, but I didn't want to believe the alternative.

"Now you really are being insulting. I'm you need to go before I say something we'll both regret."

"Layla." I reached out for her, already regretting how badly this had gone, but she brushed my hands away.

"I think now is probably a good time for us to take a

breather. We'll deal with the fallout from what happened today and then...I don't—I don't know."

Layla wrapped her arms around her waist, but flinched when I tried to step closer. My hands dropped to my side in defeat. How had we gotten here?

There wasn't anything else I could say.

So I left.

* * *

I DROVE around for an indeterminable amount of time, taking back streets and cutoffs until I was riding on a red dirt road in the middle of nowhere. I didn't want to go home, it was too close to Layla, too tempting. My temper had already gotten the best of me and she didn't deserve it. The people who did, I was terrified to confront.

My grandfather, he'd always been a cold, hard man. It was surprising my dad had ever grown up to be the kind, warm man he was with parents like his. I couldn't go to my grandparents house, not yet. First, I needed to know if my parents had a part in this. Mom never would have gone along with it, but dad—he didn't really grow a spine until he met her. Had he knuckled under to grandmother's machinations? I didn't want to think so, and I had to know.

Somehow, I made it back to their hotel room. I knocked and Mom answered the door. Her hair was down, her face scrubbed clean. I glanced at my phone and the time illuminated: 8:05.

My parents were early to bed, early to rise people, so they were getting ready to go to sleep.

"Do you have a second?" I asked. "I'm sorry it's so late."

Mom gave me a warm smile. "Of course, honey. What's wrong? You look terrible. Are you okay?"

"I'm fine. Is Dad around? I have something to talk to you both about."

"You're scaring me. Peter! Peter, it's Dash. Can you come out here for a second?"

"Naomi, you don't need to shout the whole place down. I'm right here." He came out of the bathroom of their suite, his tie loose around his neck and his suit missing the jacket, which hung around the back of a chair. "Dash, what is it?"

"He said he has to talk to us about something."

"Well, come in. Do you want something to drink?" Dad asked.

"No, thanks. I'm fine."

Mom hovered by the door as I went inside. "What do you need to talk to us about, honey?"

"It's about grandmother. Dad—" My throat constricted on the words. "Dad, did you know anything about her bribing the girl I was seeing to stay away from me? The truth, please."

"Bribing? What the hell are you talking about?" Dad's face flushed with anger. "I don't know anything about bribery."

"Jessica?" Mom asked.

"No, not Jessica. Her name is Layla. She was a student of mine. I went to school with her."

"Was a student?"

"I'll explain," I said to Mom. Then I turned back to Dad. "Did you?"

"Of course not! I haven't heard a word about it and frankly, I'm insulted that you'd believe she'd do such a thing. She loves you."

"Peter," Mom broke in, trying to alleviate the growing tension. "Don't get upset."

"Don't get upset? He's accusing my mother—"

"You say that like she didn't show up to our wedding dressed in black like it was a funeral, Peter. This is our son, he deserves our trust." She turned back to me. "Tell us what happened."

I sat on the edge of their bed and told them everything. From meeting Layla at the beginning of the semester, to an abbreviated version of our relationship, and ending with our argument from a few hours before. The longer I talked, the more disgusted I felt with myself.

She'd told me she loved me and the first thing I did was turn her away.

CHAPTER TWENTY-FIVE

LAYLA

MS. JENSEN LOOKED the same as she did at the beginning of the semester, except this time her lipstick was a bright orange-red to match her festive sweater instead of the deep pink. Her mousy hair was in its customary bun and there was a pencil tucked behind her ear.

"Well," she said, then paused, sipped coffee that had gone cold. "Well," she said again.

I wondered how many other times she'd have to say it before her vocabulary would expand.

"I must say I didn't think I'd see you again so quickly, and over such unpleasant business." Ms. Jensen clucked her tongue, then shuffled a stack of papers. "I'm sorry to say that considering, well, considering, that you won't be able to resume the business ethics class for the rest of the semester." She paused, adjusted her glasses and then studied me over the rim. "Of course, when we took into account your grade point average and your academic records, we decided make an exception on a one-time-only basis."

I straightened in the creaky leather seat. "I'm sorry? What do you mean?"

It had been a week since my blowup with Dash. I hadn't spoken to my mother—who surely thought her silent treatment was punishment rather than the reward it was. My sister spent most of every day alternating between calling, texting, and showing up at my classes. I'd blocked her number and pretended she was a stranger.

According to her, I should forgive my mother for her latest transgression. Mom only called me stupid because she was so upset about the bad decisions I was making. She didn't really mean it.

The one person I hadn't heard from, was Dash.

Now that the dust had settled, I didn't know where we stood. I hurt him, that I accepted, but he knew me. He should have trusted me.

Otherwise everything we went through was for nothing.

I realized Ms. Jensen was speaking, so I pushed Dash from my mind and tried to focus on what she was saying. "If you wanted, that is."

"What?" I said and flushed. "I'm sorry, can you repeat that?"

She smiled. "I said considering your academic record and the fact that there was no proof Mr. Hampton showed you any sort of preference whatsoever, the administration will allow you to repeat the course next semester—with a different professor, naturally."

This should have been good news.

It could have been so much worse.

I could still finish both degrees on time as though nothing had happened. If I so desired, with a little placating, I could even convince my mother everything would be fine. By placating, I mean I'd need to take that finance position she was so all-fired about. Meaning I wouldn't have any time at all to participate in any showings or work on my pieces. It would mean giving up a part of me that felt as vital as breathing.

"No," I said, and it was as though the word unlocked something inside of me. "No, I don't think so."

"No?" Ms. Jensen repeated. "Honey, I understand it's disheartening to have to repeat a course, but if you don't, then you won't be able to complete the requirements for the business portion of your degree."

I already felt lighter. Free. "Be that as it may, I don't wish to repeat the course. I'm still okay to graduate with the degree in art with a minor in education, though, right?"

Ms. Jensen shuffled through her papers, her cheeks a little pink. "Well, of course, I suppose if that's what you want. It just seems silly to have done all that work and not receive credit for it."

"It does, doesn't it? I could have saved us both some time if I'd realized what I wanted in the first place. Excuse me," I said and got to my feet. "There's something else I need to take care of. Have a wonderful break, Ms. Jensen."

A few months ago, I'd walked out of her office weitht he weight of the world on my shoulders. I'd been pursing a degree I didn't even want for a mother who only cared how it reflected on her. If I'd told her no years ago, I would have never been in this mess.

Then again, if it weren't for her, I wouldn't have crossed paths, and hypothetical swords, with Dash again.

As I walked to my car from the admin building, I took out my phone and considered calling him. I wanted to apologize, for everything, but I wasn't sure what, exactly, I'd say that could bridge the gap between everything that had happened.

Instead of reaching out to Dash, my fingers keyed in the number for my mother instead. She'd be overjoyed to hear from me—but only because it meant that she'd won and I'd broken the silence first.

"Hello?"

She answered on the first ring, sounding slightly breathless. I'd put money on the fact that she'd been waiting for my call and she'd run to her phone the second she heard it ring.

"Hey, Mom," I said. My voice was steady, sure, but I felt more vulnerable than I had in a long time. Vulnerable, but immovable. For so long, I'd tried to be the daughter she wanted. I did everything she asked, even if doing so meant losing parts of myself.

"Layla. To what do I owe the pleasure?" she asked.

I could imagine her in her office, leaned back in her desk chair with a satisfied smile on her face. I'd seen the same smile several times before—it was the one she wore when she got her way. Even thinking about it made my stomach tight with anxiety.

"I wanted to thank you for everything that you've done for me." Her tone of surprised satisfaction made my mouth twist in revulsion. "Thank you for showing me how little I meant to you. Without you, it never would have been so easy to tell you that I no longer need your help. I've dropped the Business Ethics class, which means I will be ineligible to graduate with the business portion of my degree. I've already informed Kragen's that I'm not interested in the internship. I've also spoken with the financial aid office, and I'll be applying for student loans next semester. So your threat about owning my apartment and essentially my life is now moot."

"After everything I've done for you, how dare you treat me this way?" she screeched in my ear. "You're going to fall flat on your face without my help and don't you dare come running to me when you do."

At the start of the semester, facing life without my family as a safety net would have terrified me. Defying my mother had been unthinkable. But after everything that's happened, I've realized life isn't worth living if you aren't doing what you love. It may be selfish to live on my terms, but I've been selfless long enough.

"If that's how you feel, I understand. I wish you the best and I hope you find happiness. I know I will."

My answer was a click. Somehow, I wasn't surprised. Disappointed, a little hollow inside, but not surprised.

I ached a little at the potential loss of my sister. She'd always been my mother's second-in-command, and I'd never really gotten to know her as a sister, just a flying monkey my mother would send when she didn't get me to do something she wanted. I hoped with a little space and time, maybe she would change, but I wasn't holding my breath.

I didn't think about either of them as I drove back to my apartment. With the radio cranked up, I blotted out all of my thoughts by singing along with Miley Cyrus' Party in the U.S.A.

Ember and Charlie were already waiting for me in my apartment. It wasn't a Tuesday, so they'd brought a couple twelve packs, tape, and boxes.

"I had these extra from my move last year," Charlie said as she handed me an ice cold beer. "I never got around to throwing them away, but I guess that's a good thing."

"It's not a good thing," Ember complained. "I can't believe both of you are just deserting me. Some friends."

Since my mom was officially no longer footing the bill for my apartment, I had to find somewhere more affordable. I'd applied for a full-time job with the art charity and had my fingers crossed I'd get it. It wouldn't pay much, but what it didn't cover I would supplement with what scholarships I could scrounge up and use student loans as a last resort.

"We see Charlie just as much as we did before she moved out," I reasoned, then laughed as Ember fervently shook her head.

"That's grossly untrue. She works back to back shifts all the time. Before we could see her like that," she snapped her fingers for emphasis, "but now we basically have to make an appointment. Mark my words, it'll be the same when you leave. All I'll have left is Tripp." She made a face.

"Oh, that's such a travesty," Charlie said with a giggle. "Truly, it's torture. How many abs does he have? I saw him lift his shirt last year during playoffs and I swear I counted at least twenty."

Ember threw a towel she'd been folding at Charlie's face. "For the last time we're just friends. I'm with Chris."

"For now," Charlie and I said at the same time, then share a smile. These two—they were better than any man.

"Whatever. Are you two going to pack or are you just going to sit there and run your mouths?"

"I think we're going to run our mouths while we watch you pack," I suggested.

"I'll remember this." Ember began throwing towels and washcloths into a bag willy nilly at Charlie's burst of laughter. "Next year, when it's my turn to move, I'm going to sit back with my feet up, mark my words."

"Sure, sure. I don't think you'll ever leave your apartment." Her face fell a little and I reminded myself that I wasn't the only one with problems. "I think you need another beer as much as I do," I said and grabbed her a fresh one.

"Are you going to tell us what you decided to do about Dash?" Ember said in a clear bid to change the subject.

I sipped my drink and considered. "Maybe... once we finish packing."

They both threw towels at my head.

CHAPTER TWENTY-SIX

DASH

"YOU'RE A GOOD MAN, Dash. I'm sorry to have to do this, but it's university policy."

Professor Michaels stood at the door to my office and watched as I packed. Official policy mandated suspension and immediate termination for grad students who fraternized with their students, but as there wasn't concrete evidence that my relationship with Layla went beyond one kiss he witnessed, I was given the termination and advised to steer clear of applying to any other T.A. positions.

It could have been worse.

I had one more semester before I graduated, anyway. And I didn't need the money, although the experience was useful.

"Don't sweat it, professor. I understand. Thank you for going to bat for me. I appreciate it."

"I wish I could do more, but my hands are tied. You'll let me know if you need anything? I'll be in my office."

"Of course, sir. Thanks again."

He nodded, rapped his knuckles on the doorjamb, then left me to my thoughts.

After the conversation with my parents I'd gone home, painfully aware of how close it was to Layla's. I was too consumed by guilt and fury to be in the right frame of mind to face her. Especially considering I hadn't figured out how to confront my grandmother.

After I finished packing up my office, I planned to drive over to my grandparents place on the way home and talk to them. Even if I had no clue what I was going to say.

I worked steadily during the afternoon, clearing out the bookshelves, the mini fridge, and then finally, my desk. It wasn't until I sat down in my chair that I noticed the book sitting on the center of my blotter. I knew what it was the moment I laid eyes on it.

It was a first edition copy of The Hobbit. The cover was bound in a deep teal with gold foil and filagree. I opened the cover and confirmed the publication date. Inside was a piece of paper. I recognized the handwriting from papers I'd assigned in our class.

In Layla's neat penmanship were the words:

There is some good in this world, and it's worth fighting for.
    - J.R.R. Tolkein

Beneath it, she added:

I think you're worth fighting for.

Before I could jump to my feet to race home to her, there was a knock at my door. For a split second, I was swamped by pure joy thinking it was Layla coming to see my reaction to her gift. I stood, still holding the book, but it wasn't Layla waiting for me.

It was my grandmother.

"Dashiel," she said primly.

My mouth firmed and a white-hot bolt of rage shot through me. "Grandmother," I replied. "What are you doing here?"

She stepped inside, closed the door. "You haven't been answering my calls."

"There was a reason for that."

She lifted a brow. "I assumed so. That's why I came to speak with you in person, like an adult."

I barked out a laugh. "Interesting."

"What?" she asked.

"It's interesting that you're suggesting we should treat each other like adults."

"And what is that supposed to mean?"

I gripped the back of my chair to keep myself focused and to steady my twitching hands. "You know what I'm talking about." Despite my fury, my voice was deadly calm.

"Really, Dash, I don't have time for these games."

"You offered Layla Tate money to stay away from me."

I already knew she wasn't going to cop to what she'd done unless she was confronted directly. It was disappointing to realize how similar she was to Layla's mother. No wonder the two of us got along so well... relatively speaking.

A parade of emotions washed over her face. Shock. Anger. Denial. Then she cleared her expression and affected a mask of sorrow. If I hadn't been watching her so closely, I wouldn't have believed it.

"You'd believe that girl over me?"

"That girl is a beautiful, kind, genuine person. Which you would know if you spent two seconds getting to know her."

"I don't have to get to know her to know who she is. She's exactly like your mother. Money-hungry and only interested in what she can leech from you."

I shook my head. "You're delusional. You'd rather have me with Jessica, who would dance on my grave to inherit my portfolio, than with than Layla, who genuinely cares about me. What is wrong with you?" I asked, exasperated.

"The only thing wrong with me is caring too much for my family, which goes unappreciated. I won't speak anymore about this, Dashiel, and if you want to have a place in our lives, you'll stay away from that girl and understand that when I do something, it comes from a place of love, because I care about you."

I almost believed the tears, the watery voice. Except her eyes were completely devoid of emotion. The pulse beating in her throat was steady. She could have been at a spa for all the genuine emotion she showed.

"If you cared about me, you never would have interfered."

244

The tears dried. Her voice hardened. "You better watch how you speak to me Dashiel Hampton."

"I don't think I will. The men in this family have let you run over them for far too long, and I won't let you ruin the best thing that's ever happened to me."

This time, the shock in her expression was real. "You'd choose her over your own family?"

I leaned across the desk, pressing my hands into its surface. The gold foil from the book glinted in the corner of my eyes, solidifying my resolve. "When my family lies and manipulates me? I'd choose Layla, fight for her, every. Time."

Grandmother straightened, looked down her nose. "You're going to regret this. Don't come crawling to me when she uses and discards you, Dash. I won't want to hear it."

She left and shut the door quietly. A Hampton didn't make a scene. It must have really peeved her when news spread about my relationship with Layla. Bad press wasn't acceptable. Apparently deceit and exploitation were much more tolerable.

I finished packing in the ringing silence of my grandmother's departure with the copy of The Hobbit catching my eye every few seconds. It sat in the passenger seat of my car as I drove home. Without thinking, I took the elevator to Layla's floor and my feet carried me directly to her door. I knocked, but she didn't answer.

I tried knocking again. No answer.

Her phone went straight to voicemail when I tried to call.

After twenty minutes, I gave up. I'd try again in the morning. And the next day, and the next day until she answered.

Because she was right.

We were worth fighting for.

I made my way back to my floor with renewed determination, already coming up with a plan to win her back. I was going to go the whole nine, flowers, chocolates, trips to her favorite art galleries and enough orgasms to leave her limp and sated for the rest of her life. All she had to do was give me another chance.

I wouldn't fuck it up.

I got out of the elevator on my floor, but I was looking down at my phone, texting Layla for the third time.

So I didn't see her standing at my front door until I nearly bumped into her.

She grabbed onto my arms to keep from being bowled over, but our feet tangled and we went tumbling down.

"Oof," Layla said as I landed on top of her. "Were you trying to turn me into a pancake?"

I steadied myself, raising up on my forearms to keep my weight from crushing her. "If you'd answer your phone once in a while, I wouldn't have run into you."

"I packed my phone charger, and I don't know which frigging box it's in or I would have answered my phone," she growled.

"Packed away? What do you mean packed away?"

"It's where you put things into boxes to make it easier to move them," she said slowly.

"Why are you packing?"

Layla scowled up at me. "Do we really have to have this

conversation in the middle of the hallway while you're squishing me to death?"

I got to my feet and helped her up. "Now speak."

"I'm not a dog, Dash. Why do you always have to boss me around?"

Shoving my hands through my hair, I nearly growled. I missed this?

With exaggerated care, I opened the door to my apartment and waved her inside. "I suppose asking you to sit would be outside of the question?" She sent me a scathing look and spun on her heel to leave. I caught her arm and said, "I'm kidding. Kidding! I promise. No more jokes."

I'd left my box of stuff from the office in my car, but I'd carried the copy of The Hobbit upstairs with me. When we'd crashed into each other it had gone flying. While she took a seat on the couch, I retrieved the book from where it had landed by my door.

Holding it up as I went inside, I said, "I guess by fight for me, you really meant fight *with* me."

"Dash," she said in a warning tone, but there was a hint of a smile shining from her eyes.

I sat beside her on the couch and took her hands in mine. She angled her body to face me, a wave of vulnerability creeping into her expression. "I was just at your apartment to talk to you. I guess we both had the same idea. Why are you packing?"

She looked down at our hands. "I blew my mom off and she basically cut me out of her life. I can't afford to live alone for next semester so I signed a lease with a couple other roommates until summer when I can figure something else out."

After kissing her fingers and pulling her in for a hug, I said into her hair, "I'm so sorry it came to that, but I'm proud of you. So fucking proud. She didn't deserve you. You're an amazing person, Lay. Right down to the bone. If she couldn't see that, then screw her."

She pulled back, and a tear leaked from her eye. I brushed it away with a knuckle. "Thank you. I know that's true. It's just hard because she's my mom."

"I understand. I wish I didn't, but I do."

"What about your grandmother?" she asked hesitantly.

"Before we get into that, I just want to apologize for the way I reacted. I was wrong. I know you, Layla, and I should have trusted you. I will trust you, from now on. For a long time the people around me have used me for their own means and even though I knew you would never do something like that, it was a knee-jerk reaction. I hope you know I'll spend every day for as long as you'll let me stay around making it up to you."

Her hands came to my shoulders and my eyes closed at how good it felt to have her touching me again. How right. "I understand how hard it is to be faced with the truth about your own family. If it weren't for you, I never would have come to realize exactly how bad mine were. I just hate that I had to come between you. I hope your parents understood."

The fear in her eyes had me pulling her close. "They did. My dad didn't, at first, but my mom has been putting up with my grandmother for a long time and didn't hesitate to stand up for me. And you didn't come between anyone. My grandmother made her choices. You didn't do anything wrong."

"It feels so good to hear you say that. I was worried you were going to tell me to take a hike." She sighed as she settled into me and I wondered if there was a more perfect feeling than having her in my arms.

"That wasn't what I was planning on saying," I told her.

"What were you going to say?"

I tipped her chin up with a finger and smiled. "That you're worth fighting for, too."

TWO YEARS AFTER GRADUATION, I'd never sold a piece at a gallery. I'd never become a household name as an artist. Hell, even my Etsy page did a minimal amount of business. I guess my mother had been right in assuming my art degree would never rake in the bucks.

But I couldn't be happier.

As I tidied the little garden behind the sweet yellow cottage Dash and I rented, I felt full to bursting. Radiant as the sun. If Dash didn't get home soon, I would explode with the news.

Brushing my hands off on the little apron I wore when I puttered around the garden, I surveyed my work with a keen eye. The dainty pansies and perky petunias danced in a gentle spring breeze. Tomorrow, I'd finish the darling little humming-bird feeders I'd been working on and I'd hang them in the ancient oak that towered over our backyard like a sentinel.

A tortoiseshell cat I'd named Tiger twisted around my

ankles as I gathered my supplies and packed them away in the garden shed. When I shooed her away, she scampered off to chase a pair of butterflies flittering around my lantana plants. Dash had surprised me with the kitten after I won an award last year from my employer.

Rookie Teacher of the Year.

I still couldn't believe it.

Not only that I'd found my niche, my passion, but that it hadn't been in the avenue I expected at all. I suppose it was the student teaching that I'd been required to do for my education minor. The semester after I dropped my business class, I'd decided to fill the extra time with education courses. I loved them almost as much as I loved art, which had come as a surprise to me.

I never would have considered it if it hadn't been for Dash.

At the sound of the door opening and closing, Tiger's ears perked up and her tale flicked three times in rapid succession. When footsteps echoed, she scrambled out of the lantana bushes, up the back steps and disappeared into the dining room. Moments later, I could hear the low rumble of Dash's voice greeting her.

Tiger had been a gift for me, but Dash was her true love.

I couldn't blame her.

He was mine, too.

Noting a flower that must have gotten uprooted when Tiger was chasing the butterflies, I squatted down to pack it more securely into the soil. When I finished and looked up, I found

Dash sitting on the top step of the deck, the kitten purring contentedly in his arms.

Like he had done almost every day since that fateful day in his class, he simply took my breath away.

Dash was handsome no matter what he wore, but the suits were my favorite. I was ever so thankful that he was required to wear one to work Monday through Friday. I liked seeing them on him, but I also enjoyed taking them off him.

Crossing the garden, I bent down and kissed his lips as the kitten settled into his arms. "How was work?" I asked, already feeling a little breathless and wondering how quickly I could convince him to make a detour to the bedroom.

"Dad's on a tear. His opponent is tough this year."

Despite all the protests he'd made, Dash had gone into politics, though not at the pressure of his family. His parents had told him repeatedly that whatever he decided to do, they would support him.

It turned out that without the constant pushing from his grandmother, he actually enjoyed helping with his father's campaign. After completing his MBA, Dash joined his father as a campaign manager, and he never looked back.

It was a side benefit that his grandmother wasn't allowed to attend any events, and she frequently made her displeasure known. Not that anyone cared.

My mother hadn't contacted me since the day she disowned me. She wasn't missed. Delia, on the other hand, had since been to therapy and we were slowly rebuilding our relationship. It's hard and awkward, but she's making the effort, so I am, too. I'm cautiously optimistic, but I keep my ears tuned for any nonsense about mending fences with my mother.

"He'll win. Hampton's always do," I said.

"That's because we have excellent taste." Dash said, drawing me into his lap, displacing a disgruntled Tiger. "I have something for you."

"I have something to tell you, too."

Dash smiled patiently. "You first."

The news burst forth. "Liam and Charlie are having a baby!"

He winced a little at the volume of my voice. "That's wonderful. I bet they're excited."

"She couldn't wait to tell everyone. Now you, what's your news?"

"We may have to wait to tell them so we don't steal their thunder, but maybe you can keep a secret."

He placed a package in my lap and I tore into it with the enthusiasm of a child.

It was a pristine copy Charlotte's Web. Inside was a note.

"You have been my friend," replied Charlotte, "That in itself is a tremendous thing."
  - E.B. White

Below that it said:

Layla,

There's nothing I would like more than to spend the rest of my
life arguing with you.

Marry me?

Attached to the note was a ring.

Keep reading for a sneak peek at the next book in the
series...Friends with Benefits!

FRIENDS WITH BENEFITS - CHAPTER ONE

EMBER

I WAS in the home improvement store trying to figure out which carpet to buy to replace the one's my sisters had ruined when I got the text message.

I ignored it for a few minutes as I decided between the sand-castle and brilliant beige. The last thing I should be doing is putting *more* stainable light-colored carpet in their room, but they were the only two options in my price-range and my budget was already stretched to the max. My parents should be attending to this particular responsibility, but asking them to do anything responsible was like trying to pluck a star from the sky: impossible.

"How much is this one?" I asked, pointing to the beige. The clerk stretched to check the printouts as I dragged out my phone to read the text.

At first, my heart lifted at the From: indicator. It was Chris, my boyfriend who was away at college in Miami. It had been a couple days since I heard from him and although I wanted to talk to him more often, he'd made it a point to let me know I was smothering him, so I backed off.

Apparently, I hadn't backed off far enough.

CHRIS: Hey pretty lady. Wassup?

It should have pleased me to hear from him, but an indescribable weight seemed to take up residence on my shoulders. Anxeity bubbled in my stomach. All I wanted was for us to work out. Our relationship had become more work than anything else, but that's what relationships were—or so I told myself. If I kept working at this would, it would pay off.

ME: Getting carpet for the twins' room. How are you?

Somehow, my relationship with the man who I thought I loved had turned into a carnival reflection of itself. I didn't recognize it when I looked in the mirror. Chris and I had met when we were in high school, then reconnected when we were at the same community college. I was training to be an EMT, he was finishing prerequisites to transfer to a four-year university. To be honest, I'd had a crush on him for as long as I could remember and when he reciprocated interest, I thought I was the luckiest girl in the world.

It had been a long time since I thought I was the luckiest girl in the world.

Ever since things had gotten more serious and the time began to draw near for me to either stay in Tallahassee or join him in Miami, he'd begun to retreat. The more I tried to make it work, the more he pulled away. In my heart, I knew what that meant, but I didn't quite know how to give up hope.

It didn't matter. Reading his text told me all I needed to know about our future together. As the words began to sink in, my tongue went as dry as the Mojave and my thoughts blurred together.

CHRIS: Look, I think I need to be upfront about something with you. I don't want to hurt you, but I've met someone. I thought I should tell you.

My fingers went numb from where they clutched at the phone. Even though I had an inkling it was coming, the reality was so much worse than anything I could have dreamt up. My vision went white and dramatic though it was, I couldn't seem to catch my breath.

I'd never been the type of girl who went gaga over any guy, but I guess there was a first time for everything.

It shouldn't hurt so much to have my suspicions confirmed. I hadn't wanted to say my fears out loud, afraid that it would make them too real.

But here it was, in black and white. The undeniable truth.

The guy I'd loved, the one I'd trusted and believed in for so long wasn't who I thought he was.

The poor clerk who was reading off measurements, colors, and prices goggled after me as I dropped the other supplies I'd been considering in the shopping cart and then abandoned it in the middle of the aisle.

Normally, I loved this store. I love the possibilities of it. The little apartment I rented for my family wasn't in the best shape and fixing it up was one of the most rewarding things about my somewhat dismal life. But suddenly the sky-high shelves of paint chips and caulk didn't feel reassuring. Instead, the winding aisles became a maze from which there was no escape.

I texted a response blindly. I was sure to read it back later and regret it, but if the only weapons I had were words, I wanted to aim for his heart and make them hurt.

ME: Then I guess all the promises you made about wanting to be with me forever, all the times you said you loved me. All those were just lies? I'm not a perfect person, but I deserved better than this. I shouldn't be as surprised as I am, but actually believed the bullshit you spun to me about it being us

against the world. Lose my number. I don't ever what to hear from you again.

As tears flooded my vision, I blocked his number and navigated through the aisles to the front door. I don't know how I made it back to the apartment complex without wrapping my car around a pole, but I did. Sheer will, I supposed. All those late nights driving an ambulance, high on adrenaline must have paid off.

An indeterminable amount of time later, I found myself in the shower, the cold spray beating down on my naked body and hot tears streaming down my cheeks. I didn't know a person could hurt so much. It felt like I was dying, except there was nothing I knew in my repertoire of life-saving skills that could resuscitate me.

I don't know how long I sat there, wallowing in the self-pity. It could have been minutes, but it felt like years. The water began to run cold, although I could barely feel it. My brain seemed to have disconnected from my body. It was probably a good thing. The flashes of pain that radiated down to the marrow of my bones were almost too much to handle.

I'd never believed in broken hearts. Get over it, I'd think to myself when friends of mine would go through a break up. Even when Liam and Charlie or Layla and Dash had split, grated for a short time, I didn't think it would be so bad. They'd gotten back together, after all. I'd been with Chris so long, it had never occurred to me what would happen when we broke up. Not even when things started to get so rocky a couple months ago.

More fool me.

My laugh echoed off the dingy subway tiles and I peeled myself off of the tub to turn off the water. My hair matted to my head, but I couldn't find the energy to care. Any concern aside from surviving had leaked out of me in the torrent of tears and seeped down the drain.

The twins still had another couple hours at school. Mom was probably off with whatever bum she'd hooked up with over the weekend and my father, who didn't seem to care who she slept with, was no doubt glued to a barstool down the road at his favorite haunt.

I was alone.

I doubled over as the implication stabbed through me.

I was alone.

I had my family, but they were more of a responsibility. I'd get through this for them. I had my friends, but they had their own lives and I didn't want to burden them, not yet. It wasn't in my nature to lean on others. I provided for my family, worked myself to the bone without any help from my deadbeat parents. I would survive this, even if it didn't feel like it at the moment.

For now, it felt like the pain encapsulated everything, blotted out my surroundings and contracted until I was only the dull ache in my chest. I staggered to my bedroom, a towel wrapped loosely around my body and water dripping from my saturated hair onto the worn wood floors. I didn't care. I couldn't scrounge up the energy to do more than throw myself onto the bed and pull the mussed covers around me.

My phone was hauntingly silent, which only made the tears fall harder. There were no social media notifications. No emails. I knew, somewhere deep down in my soul, that he wouldn't try reaching out that way.

He'd found someone else.

I'd supported him through his father's death the year before. When he didn't think he could pass his finals after the funeral, I stayed up after two double shifts and helping the twins through a stomach virus to quiz him. For his birthday, I'd driven down and taken him to his favorite restaurant even though I was barely making enough money to pay rent and support my sisters.

I would have done anything for him.

I *did* do anything for him.

Was that where I went wrong? Had I made it *too* easy? Was one of those women who got boring in a relationship because I wasn't exciting or sexy enough?

My thoughts spiraled down a black hole and I covered my face with a pillow until I'd cried myself dry. I must have dozed off at times because a sudden realization would jerk me awake, then it would start all over again.

One day, I told myself. I'd give him one day of being upset, then I'd push it away, bury it deep, and never think of this—or him—again.

It was wishful thinking, considering we'd been together for a long time, but the thought of feeling this way forever tempted to give way to a despair so all-encompassing, I was afraid I wouldn't survive it.

The front door slammed and pattering feet bounded into the apartment. The twins were home. I shot to my feet and winced as a headache throbbed insistently behind my eyes.

"Ember!" one of them called.

"Shh!" said the other. "What if she's sleeping?"

The first scoffed. "She's never sleeping."

It made me laugh. They always made me laugh. Raising them should have never fallen on my shoulders, but they were the lights of my life. The sound of their innocent debate drew me from the shelter of blankets and I glanced at my phone to find it blinking 3:24 p.m. I must have fallen asleep after my crying jag.

"Do you think we should check on her? What if she's sick?" The second asked.

"Maybe we should get the therbombiter, Tillie." Which meant it was Molly speaking.

"Do you know how to use it?" Molly asked with clear interest.

"Sure, all you do is stick it in her mouth and push the button. I'll get it from the medicine cabinet. You get a glass of water and the throw-up bowl in case she's stomach sick."

Matilda Leanne was the oldest of my twin sisters—by a whole twenty minutes. It may as well have been twenty years for how she bossed around her younger sister, Molly Elizabeth.

The patter of their feet echoed down the hall and I decided to wait for them to return to see what they would do. Besides, I didn't have the energy to get back to my feet quite yet. As I contemplated getting up, I heard them return.

"You knock, Tillie," Molly said.

"No, you knock," Tillie replied.

"You always tell me what to do," Molly whined, but it was followed by a rapping sound.

"Ember are you 'kay? It's us."

My face felt like I'd been repeatedly punched as I smiled and raised my voice to say, "Come in." I wiped away any evidence of tears and tried in vain to straighten my hair and look like I hadn't been crying for ours.

Two orange-headed girls of six bounded in my room. Tillie's curls were soft waves that floated around her shoulders. Molly's were tight ringlets that bounced with each step. They were terrors and the lights of my life.

"We brought you some water and a therbombiter. Are you sick?" Tillie asked as she sat on the side of the bed. Molly climbed up and around to my other side.

"Just a little tired," I said, edging around the truth. "The water will help."

I took the glass Molly offered, amazed she hadn't spilled it in her climb up. The water was tepid, but wet, and after crying for hours I felt like a wrung out rag. I was probably a little dehydrated.

The girls stared at me expectantly. "Thank you, babies," I said with a squeeze. "This is perfect. Do you have homework?"

Tillie wagged her finger at me and Molly giggled. "No work

until you feel better. You always let us watch T.V. when we don't feel good."

I didn't have it in me to argue. Homework could wait. I pulled the girls close, sighing as their little bodies fitted into my side.

Who needed a man when I had them?

DEAR READER

Thank you so much for getting to know Layla and Dash!

I sincerely hope you enjoyed reading this book as much as I enjoyed writing it. If you did, I would greatly appreciate a short review on Amazon or your retailer. Reviews are crucial for any author, and even just a line or two can make a huge difference.

I look forward to reading your thoughts!

XOXO,

Nicole

Also in the Series:

Frenemies (Layla & Dash)

Friends with Benefits (Tripp & Ember)

ACKNOWLEDGMENTS

This book, like so many of its predecessors, wouldn't have been possible without some very patient and supportive people.

To my Knockouts. You have put up with my flighty butt for years on end. You've supported me through everything. Your enthusiasm and patience has meant the world to me. This one is absolutely for you!

To my daughter. I've spent the last week chained to my computer to finish this book. It meant time away from you. Time I won't get back. I don't take that lightly. I hope you know everything I do is for you, and I hope you understand how much you mean to me.

To Alana. I continue to be grateful for your helping hand and your sympathetic ear.

To each and every blogger who helps spread the word. Thank you for your tireless dedication and unwavering support!

Thank you to Octopi Covers for your amazing design work

on this series. These books continue to remain some of my favorite covers.

Thank you Karen Hrdlicka from Barren Acres Editing for being the best a girl could ask for!

To Melissa Fisher, Cindy Camp, Vera Green, MIchell Hall Casper, Terry Lawrence, Rhonda Brant, and Jessica Layos Nielson. I can't thank you enough for beta reading Frenemies from the ground up. I'd be lost without you.

Last but not least, thank you to each and every one of you for reading!

ABOUT THE AUTHOR

 **Nicole Blanchard** is the *New York Times* and *USA Today* bestselling author of gritty romantic suspense and heart-warming new adult romance. She and her family reside in the south along with their two spunky Boston Terriers, two spunky cats, and a hamster with a Houdini problem. Visit her website www.authornicoleblanchard.com for more information or to subscribe to her newsletter for updates on sales and new releases.

f facebook.com/authornicoleblanchard

🐦 twitter.com/blanchardbooks

📷 instagram.com/authornicoleblanchard

a amazon.com/Nicole-Blanchard

BB bookbub.com/authors/nicole-blanchard

ALSO BY NICOLE BLANCHARD

First to Fight Series

Anchor

Warrior

Survivor

Savior

Honor

Box Set: Books 1-5

Traitor

Operator

Aviator

Captor

Protector

Friend Zone Series

Friend Zone

Frenemies

Friends with Benefits

The Lost Planet Series

The Forgotten Commander

The Vanished Specialist

The Mad Lieutenant

Immortals Ever After Series

Deal with a Dragon

Vow to a Vampire

Fated to a Fae King

Dark Romance

Toxic

Fatal

Standalone Novellas

Bear with Me

Darkest Desires

Mechanical Hearts

www.ingramcontent.com/pod-product-compliance
Lightning Source LLC
Chambersburg PA
CBHW010818250626
47156CB00011B/3115